CARICATURE OF A COUNTESS

MELISSA SAWYER

To fil

Enjoy the story!

Melissa Sawyer

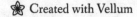

To my husband - my love, my biggest supporter, and the one who encouraged me to keep working at this book. Thank you.

CHAPTER ONE

As he walked up the steps to Lord and Lady Winslow's house, Daniel reminded himself for the third time, he never broke promises. Ever. And Iris, that crafty cousin of his, had caught him in a promise, curse her.

He handed his card, hat, and gloves to the footman at the door. The clock chimed the quarter hour. Perfect, he was late. Daniel stifled the urge to take back his hat and gloves and leave before going further into the house. Promise or no promise.

"This way, my lord." The footman's directive ended any hope of escape.

They crossed the hall and continued down the corridor towards the back of the house. Excited chatter and laughter echoed off of the polished marble floors, growing louder with every step. The footman handed his card to the butler.

"The earl of Beechingstoke."

Chatter dimmed, and the weight of dozens of eyes pressed upon Daniel. He straightened his shoulders and entered the room, searching for a friendly face in a sea of sharp-clawed mothers and their eligible daughters.

Where the devil was Iris? A thought caused a sheen to break on his forehead. What if she tricked him and wasn't even here? Oh lord, was it too late to escape?

"Beechingstoke, darling!"

Too late. The crowd parted as an elegant silver-haired lady in a fashionable primrose gown walked towards him. Daniel took comfort in the friendly call of his hostess. He caught her proffered gloved hand and bowed over it.

"Good afternoon, Lady Winslow. May I say, you are the loveliest thing in this room."

With her free hand, Lady Winslow flicked open her fan and laughed. "You'd best not let the others hear that, Beechingstoke. Artists are temperamental creatures. Belittle their work at your peril."

Daniel followed his hostess's fan. Around him, landscapes, portraits, and other artwork of all sizes lined the walls of the room. People mingled around statues of animals, busts, and figures standing on pedestals. Good lord, it was as bad as the Royal Academy Exhibition. Was he expected to spend his afternoon admiring the dabbling of aristocrats who believed that their works were masterpieces, or their protégés who were just as bad, if not worse?

Cousin or not, he was going to kill Iris for forcing him to attend.

"There you are!" Speak of the devil. Iris, his maddening cousin, pushed her way through the crowd towards him, her exquisite blue dress fluttering in her wake. She may have been short in stature, but her commanding presence and the ridiculous blue peacock feathers poking out of her brown locks bounced and made her easier to track.

"Good afternoon, Lady Redwick." Daniel kissed his cousin's cheek.

She huffed. "You're late, Beech."

"It's almost as if he chose to skulk in, show his face to us, and leave," Lady Winslow drawled.

Daniel cleared his throat. Was he that transparent? "Well, I made a promise to attend, and here I am."

Lady Winslow reached up and patted Daniel on the cheek as if he was a lad of eight instead of eight-and-twenty. "You're humouring me, but I'll allow it."

The moment their hostess dismissed them, Iris threaded her arm into his and moved him across the room.

"You must see this painting."

Daniel cocked a brow. Her tone was unnaturally loud, even for Iris. He started to speak, but she squeezed his arm, and he snapped his mouth shut. Evidently whatever they were to discuss would have to wait until they had a pretence of privacy. In this room, it was nigh on possible.

She led him to a smaller chamber at the opposite

end of the hall, stuffed with more paintings than people. This art must lack wealthy patrons or be truly atrocious if they were banished to a side room.

"Alton's been at it again."

Daniel strained to hear her quiet tone, unaware Iris could talk so softly.

"What did he do this time? Gambling debts?" Daniel's third cousin and current heir, Randolph Alton, was nothing but lazy and indolent.

The sway of the blue feather as Iris shook her head almost poked Daniel in the eye. "It's much worse. He played false with a gentleman's daughter."

Daniel's fists clenched. He abhorred those who preyed on women and then walked away once they'd had their amusements. "How is the lady? What has become of her?"

"I've seen to her welfare and that of the babe."

Daniel exhaled. Iris, he knew, was involved in a charity that created safe havens for women who had nowhere else to go. Daniel provided her with whatever funds she requested.

"I'll have my man of business look into Alton and see how we can set him straight." The last thing Daniel needed was another scandal attached to the Beechingstoke name.

"That's all I ask." Iris patted Daniel's arm, then froze. A frown flickered across her face as something behind him caught her eye. "Oh. Excuse me, Beech. There's someone I must speak with."

Alone again, Daniel shook his head and stepped

back to survey his surroundings.

What the room lacked in people, it made up for in art. Paintings and drawings filled every square inch so that it was difficult to determine the colour of the walls beneath the pieces. There were large portraits, vast landscapes, and miniature pictures, all competing for the viewer's regard. It was overwhelming. Daniel craved the sedate and orderly gallery at his estate. At least in his gallery, he could examine every painting without the others begging for his attention.

His gaze roamed desperately for something of substance to catch his eye. He had no desire to return to the larger, crowded hall, and it was still too soon to leave.

A pencil sketch inserted in a corner, almost as if it was placed there solely because it fit, captured his attention.

He sauntered across the room to get a better look. The sketch was of a young mother and baby. The mother was in profile to the artist, her hand curled protectively around her baby. In her other hand, she held a rattle. The baby's chubby fists were outstretched, reaching for the toy.

He smiled, memories floating to the surface of his mind of Iris holding one of her children in a similar position. What was something as exquisite as this doing in this room, without a place of prominence? Daniel shook his head. There was no accounting for taste.

The sound of a familiar feminine laugh in the outer chambers caught his interest. Iris rarely laughed with such gusto in public. Curious, Daniel had one last look at the sketch before seeking out his cousin. What could be so funny that she forgot herself?

Between the statues, full walls, and crush of people, Daniel struggled to maintain his composure. Glimpsing a blue feather, Daniel skirted around the edge of the room, practically knocking over a sculpture on a pedestal in his effort to find Iris.

He set the sculpture to rights, grateful that it wasn't broken, lest he be forced to purchase the ugly object, but his cousin had disappeared again. He scanned the hall, his gaze pausing on Iris before landing on a lady beside her. His breath hitched.

She was the loveliest woman he'd ever seen. A riot of russet hair was tamed with hair pins and ribbons into a semblance of respectability. Several curls danced on her nape where the skin met the top of a pale blue gown. She stood beside his cousin, slightly taller than Iris. She'd fit just under his chin.

The lady smiled at something as her gaze found his. The world melted away, sounds of debates and laughter drowned out by the pounding of his heart in his ears. Daniel took a step forward, then another. He was halfway towards her before he was aware he'd even moved.

"Beech!" Iris's happy call tore Daniel's gaze from the lady. What spell had she cast upon him? His cheeks heated. Good god, was he blushing like a school boy?

"Come meet a dear friend." Iris gestured between

them. "Lord Beechingstoke, may I present Miss Denton, the daughter of Viscount Lynd. Miss Denton, my cousin, the Earl of Beechingstoke."

Daniel bent over the offered hand. "A pleasure, Miss Denton."

"Is it?" A grin teased at her lips. "You certainly didn't think so the last time we met."

Daniel's smile faltered. He searched his memory. When would he have met this glorious woman? "I'm afraid you have me at a disadvantage."

"The Griffins' wedding breakfast." She waited expectantly.

Griffin was his best friend, and Daniel had stood up with him at the wedding three years prior. It was a small wedding breakfast, primarily made up of family and close neighbours. There were several young misses present. Griffin had insisted Daniel dance with them all.

Recognition dawned on Daniel. He'd just finished dancing with the new Mrs. Griffin and went to fetch her a drink. A young chit scarcely out of the schoolroom had collided with him, and the punch she carried had spilled all over the two of them. "You're the one who spilled punch all over me."

She bristled. "I did not! You bumped into me."

"You ought to have been more careful."

"And *you* ought to have watched where you were going."

Iris cleared her throat.

Daniel looked up to find several people were

watching them. His ears burned. It was bad enough that he was here, but he abhorred drawing attention to himself. He offered the ladies each an arm. "I'm certain there's something you wanted me to see, dear cousin..."

Iris tucked her arm in his. Miss Denton hesitated. Her eyes met his. Her lips pressed firmly together, she looped her arm into his with as little contact as possible.

Daniel listened with half an ear as Iris pointed out several pictures she thought were worth a notice. They then ambled back into the smaller chamber. Miss Denton dropped his arm the moment the crowds thinned. She clasped her hands behind her back and went to study the paintings.

"Ah, this is the one I admire." Iris pointed at the mother and baby sketch Daniel had admired earlier.

He smiled. "As did I. It is charming, unlike that one." He waved a dismissive hand at the portrait of the lady staring off into the distance, a single rose with sharp thorns pinched precariously between two fingers. "It's sentimental rubbish. The lady clearly needs to be more cautious of her attire and the flower. She'll cut herself on the thorns."

"Or perhaps it's a warning of how precarious a woman's value is in our society." Miss Denton huffed.

Daniel gaped. Did Miss Denton just discuss a woman's virtue with him, a stranger? What an odd creature. "You shock me with such a speech, madam! I don't know how you can see that."

"It's clear, Beech." Iris swept a hand at the

composition. "The flower has both beauty and danger. She's struggling to keep hold of her beauty, her reputation, but if she's not vigilant, the thorns will cut her. Just like society will cut any lady who dares not satisfy their high standards."

"Iris, you're bamming me." Daniel shook his head. "It's just a woman and a flower. The artist wants you to think more so that he'll drive up the value."

Iris clucked her tongue. "Beech, dear, that's rude."

"No, it's not." He warmed to his subject. "These artists need to find a patron and make a living. Some poor fool will overhear your commentary and snap the painting up at an inflated cost. I bet the painter, whoever he is, is rubbing his hands with glee, anticipating the sale. It doubtless has a ridiculous title, too."

Daniel stepped forward, determined to make his point to the ladies and read aloud the painting's title. "A Rose among Thorns, by S. Denton."

Iris drew in a sharp breath. Daniel stepped back from the painting to regard his cousin. Her features paled, unlike the firm set of her companion's jaw, Miss Denton.

"Oh, I say. I hope this isn't a relative, is it, Miss Denton?" Daniel rubbed the hairs that picked up on the back of his neck.

"No, my lord. S. Denton isn't a relation." Her beautiful brown eyes narrowed at him.

"Well, that's good..."

"*I* am S. Denton." She gestured from the painting

and back to herself. "This is my work. As is the sketch you and Lady Redwick were admiring."

Oh, bloody hell. Now he'd gone and done it.

Daniel cleared his throat. Heat rose up his neck, and he suspected he was blushing like a schoolboy awaiting punishment from his governess. "Miss Denton, I..."

She raised a hand, cutting off his apology. "No need to apologize, my lord. It's evident you don't understand art."

Daniel bristled at the disdain in her tone. "Who is to say someone is an expert at art? Just because you can paint doesn't make you an expert on art."

The moment the words left his mouth, Daniel knew he'd gone too far. He stepped back. Horror and bile filled his throat. How could he suggest such things to a gentlewoman? He cleared his throat. "I beg your pardon, madam. That was most uncivil of me. You are more of an authority of art than I am. Please accept my most sincere apologies."

Her colour high, Miss Denton refused to look at him. She focused her attention on Iris. "If you'll pardon me, my lady. I am feeling unwell and I wish to find my party and return home."

"Of course," Iris muttered, glaring at Daniel. "Shall I escort you to your mother before I beat my cousin?"

A laugh escaped Miss Denton's lips, and her shoulders eased. "No, I shall leave at once so you can commence your beating. Good day, my lady."

They watched her leave the room.

"Do I need to send you back to the nursery, Beech?" Iris hissed.

Daniel rubbed his face and sighed. "I doubt it will do me any good."

~

The contents of the drawer shifted and clattered as Stella yanked at it with such force she nearly pulled it off of its rail. She rummaged through its contents, pulling out a penknife, ponte-crayons, and pencils.

She sat on a stool at the mahogany drawing board, a large masculine desk that looked out of place in her otherwise feminine room. Stella adjusted the angle of the writing surface, running her hand across the smooth leather, removing anything that would mar the paper she laid atop the desk. She set her materials to her right on the ledge that extended from the right drawer.

A sharpened pencil in hand, Stella sketched several shapes. Slowly, the light lines of ovals, circles, and triangles altered, changing from shapes to a forehead, eyes, and lips. Strong masculine features escaped her pencil, settling themselves on to the page.

With a huff of air, Stella set the sheet aside and drew out a fresh one, the previous form being too elegant. It wasn't the man himself she sought to capture, but his character.

Her next attempt was better. A lip twisted into a

supercilious sneer below an exaggerated nose. The rest of the man was too strong, too handsome, too...

"Drat!"

Her pencil danced across the work surface before rolling to a stop beside an inkwell. Stella sat back on the stool and crossed her arms, surveying the drawing with a critical eye.

A sardonic Lord Beechingstoke smirked back at her.

"He must have made quite the impression on you."

Stella jumped, her hand clutching her chest. She took a deep breath to steady her racing pulse. "Must you sneak up on a person, Laurette?"

"It's not sneaking when one is expected." The door hinges of the clothes press creaked as Laurette, her maid, opened the door. "Are you wearing your pink or your green dress to dinner?"

A quick glance at the clock had Stella scrambling to tidy her desk. She'd been drawing longer than expected.

"I'll wear the green." Stella surveyed her pencil-smudged hands with a frown. She crossed the room to the pitcher and basin of water. The scent of lavender and roses teased her senses as she worked up a lather to remove all traces of her activities.

"Who is he?"

"The earl of Beechingstoke." Stella immersed her hands in the water and closed her eyes. If only she could wash away her encounter with him the same way. "He's someone worth drawing."

CHAPTER TWO

Daniel rolled his shoulders to dispel the sweat running down his spine. He longed to remove the wire mask so he could take a deep, cleansing breath, but to do so would finish off the fight.

At the signal, he resumed his stance, his right foot in front of him, left foot perpendicular and behind, knees bent. He eyed his masked opponent, determined to do better than the last round.

Daniel lunged forward, his right heel hitting the ground before his toe, the open-toe sandal smacking against the floor, his left foot hopping to catch up. His gaze narrowed as his opponent parried his attack. He shifted his blade as he riposted, sliding under Griffin's blade. Griffin dodged the hit, making a counter-riposte.

They parried and sallied back and forth across the floor, neither wanting to give the other the advantage.

"Gentlemen," the officiant called, halting the play

before stepping forward, "I believe you've both had enough for today."

Daniel lowered his foil. He bowed to Griffin and removed his gloves and mask, tossing them onto the floor. Grimacing, he handed his foil to the attendant and gestured for a towel. Rubbing the sweat from his face, he reviewed every action he had taken in the match, disgusted with himself. Under normal circumstances, his matches with Griffin were close, but the loss today was different.

And both of them knew it.

He tossed the towel into a bin, before fumbling at the buttons on the heavy fencing jacket designed to protect his torso. He dressed in silence, his thoughts moving as fast as the foil.

He adjusted his beaver hat and pulled his greatcoat around him. Daniel could no longer bear Griffin's concerned gaze as they exited the fencing master's workshop. That was the problem with good friends—they knew you too well.

The blast of a sharp, icy wind was a welcome smack in the face, forcing Daniel to collect his thoughts. The thoughts that clogged his mind, allowing Griffin to beat him.

"I've received word about Alton." Anger and frustration laced Daniel's tone as he recalled the enlightening meeting with his man of business earlier in the day. "Besides causing harm to a gentlewoman, he's racking up debts and causing a general nuisance.

I've spent years fixing the Beechingstoke name, and I'll be damned if he brings us down again."

Griffin blew out a low whistle. "What do you plan to do?"

Daniel cleared his throat. He explored several options, including several that weren't legal. "I'm going to remove Alton from the succession."

The silence grew heavy as they continued to walk. In a low voice, his friend asked, "Will you be *removing* Alton?"

Daniel barked a laugh. "I'm not going to have him killed, Griffin." He shook his head. "I plan to marry. An heir and a spare, and Alton's out of succession."

"Marry? Do you have anyone in mind?"

Daniel scratched the back of his neck, hesitating. "I hoped you could help me."

"I can't marry you," Griffin deadpanned. "It's just not done, old fellow."

Daniel rolled his eyes. "You've danced with most of the debutantes and are on friendly terms with their families. I suspect you know more about the debutantes than any of the patronesses at Almack's. I've a short list of requirements—you just need to give me names."

"What about love? Affection?" Griffin stopped walking, his tone grave. "Marriage is supposed to be forever. You'll want both."

"Will I?" Daniel didn't hide the bitter tone in his voice. "What good has love done anyone?"

Griffin winced, pain flashing on his face. Guilt rose

as Daniel remembered how much Griffin had loved his bride, Grace, who died shortly after their wedding.

"Sorry," Daniel muttered, the words hollow to his own ears.

Love in a marriage was not something Daniel wanted or planned. A memory of his parents' voices raised in a heated quarrel sprang to mind. They were always angry with one another. He took a steadying breath, squashing the bitter memory. Love was too volatile of an emotion.

Daniel cleared his throat. "I've also asked Iris for help. I thought between the two of you, we can find a decent lady. She needs to be respectable, biddable, and capable of producing heirs. Preferably not a cit. I don't need money, I need breeding."

"Very well." Griffin sighed, but Daniel knew he had his friend's support. "Give me a day or two, and I'll have a list for you."

Iris marched into his study two days later like a general on campaign. "Beech, I'm convinced this is one of the worst ideas I've ever heard. And the two of you have had plenty of horrible ideas."

"Delighted to see you too, Lady Redwick." Daniel smothered a grin as he and Griffin stood. Growing up together, Iris had just as many 'horrible' ideas as Daniel and Griffin. If she wasn't the instigator, she was always a willing participant.

"Don't you dare 'Lady Redwick' me," Iris warned as she pulled folded papers from her reticule. "I'll give the children sweets and set them loose on you."

"Admit it, the brats love me, and you know it." Daniel bowed to his cousin before resuming his seat. "I am Samuel's godfather, after all."

He enjoyed his time with Iris's three small children. He'd do anything for them, and everyone knew it.

She rolled her eyes at Beech before greeting Griffin. Setting into her chair, Iris tossed the folded papers onto his desk. She tilted her head, studying him. "Are you certain you want to find a wife this way? To pick off a lady based on our recommendations? If you're worried about the earldom, there are other ways to handle Alton."

"I know what I'm doing." He'd set this idea in motion, and he wanted to see it through.

Iris scoffed. "This is nonsensical. Like something Mr. Starr would print."

"I take it you've seen one of his recent works." Daniel grimaced. He disliked caricature artists, particularly after the mockery of his parents' marriage in the scandal sheets when he was a child.

Mr. Starr was a relatively new caricature artist, his work appearing in the windows of the McInnis's Print Shop only a few months before. He was becoming as popular as James Gillray and Thomas Rowlandson. Given his incisively satirical caricatures of the ton as well as the mystery around the man's identity, he'd developed quite a following.

"I haven't," Griffin said with curiosity.

"Oh, I brought a copy with me." Iris opened her reticule, pulling out a piece of paper with a flourish.

Daniel rubbed his hand over his eyes, smothering a groan.

Iris gleefully unravelled the print and passed it to Griffin. "I think it's one of his best yet."

Daniel eyed Griffin as the man studied the drawing. Griffin raised the paper up towards Daniel and chuckled. "A nice likeness. What did you do to deserve this?"

"Nothing. And it's not me." Daniel didn't want to look at the caricature again. He knew that the sardonic, sneering gentleman looked like him. It was an unflattering image, but fortunately, just that. Not nearly as detrimental as the caricatures of his father with his peccadilloes that Daniel's schoolmates had mocked him with as a child.

He snatched the paper, folded it, and handed it back to Iris. "Put it away before I destroy it."

Iris frowned as she clutched the sheet and returned it to her reticule.

Daniel smoothed out both pieces of parchment on his desk for comparison, determined to get back to the task at hand. Both lists were brief, with several names overlapping. He glanced at the first name written by both and raised an eyebrow.

"Miss Denton?" An image of the russet-haired

beauty from the art exhibition flashed in Daniel's mind. Her sweet image soured as he remembered her words. She would make a horrible wife, wouldn't she? "Is there another Miss Denton I'm unaware of?"

Griffin and Iris exchanged grins, clearly enjoying the fact that they'd chosen the same lady as their first choice. "She's a lovely girl," Griffin told him.

"To look at, perhaps. She's opinionated and brash." Daniel scoffed. "If you think she's so sweet, then why don't you marry her?"

"She was one of Grace's cousins, but she's nothing like Grace." Griffin looked away and added in a quiet voice, "No one is."

A sense of melancholy shadowed the room like a cloud passing over the sun. It had been two years since Grace's death, but Daniel knew there were no words that could offer comfort.

"Yes, well, Miss Denton *is* lovely," Iris said, steering the discussion away from the past and back to their present task. "And she's smart and kind, and my brood likes her."

"If she has the brats' approval, she must be special," Griffin teased.

Daniel rubbed his chin. Iris did not invite just anyone to meet her children, so that was a point in Miss Denton's favour. If Miss Denton was someone Iris trusted, then Daniel could not strike her off the list.

He examined the rest of the names in front of him, determined to view the other options, hopefully, with more interesting results.

Daniel pulled a sheet of paper from his desk and copied the names that were on both lists. He hesitated before deciding to include Miss Denton. He passed the sheets back to Griffin and Iris, who examined the remaining names.

Iris grabbed the quill, striking three names that had been on Griffin's list.

"This one is a harridan, that one's all but engaged in a love match, and Miss Ives has a detestable mother." she said with a shudder.

"Would you discount a woman based on her parents?" Daniel asked, surprised.

"If the relations are intolerable, yes." Griffin glanced over Iris's list before setting it back on the table. "I bow to your superior knowledge of the families, my lady."

Iris smirked. Daniel crossed his arms. She was insufferable enough without Griffin adding more fuel to the fire. He gritted his teeth. Perhaps asking Iris for support was a foolish idea.

Forcing himself to focus on the task at hand, Daniel reviewed the list of ten remaining names. Ten potential brides. Ten potential ladies, one of whom would provide him with heirs to snatch the earldom out of Alton's grasp. Which one should he choose?

Rubbing a hand across his brow, Daniel glanced at the list again, and asked, "Which ones are good ton? Whose families are solvent and won't beggar me?"

Iris and Griffin re-examined the list, removing another five names. With finality, Iris struck off two more names, saying, "These two are nice but rather silly girls. They'd bore you to tears."

That left three names. Daniel looked at the paper and frowned. Miss Denton's name was still there, along with Lady Cecilia Montclair, whose ducal father Daniel was familiar with, and another lady he did not know.

"How do I choose from these ladies without making my intent to marry known?" Daniel asked. "I don't want to be inundated with silly chits and matchmaking mamas if it's known I'm searching for a wife."

Silence descended on the trio.

Perhaps Iris was right, not that he would tell her that; it *was* a bad idea. Daniel ran a hand through his hair. Maybe he ought to forget the whole thing.

Iris broke the silence. "Redwick and I will host a dinner party. We can invite the ladies and their families. You can meet them and decide who's the most suitable."

"I still think you should just marry Miss Denton and be done with all this nonsense," Griffin grumbled.

Daniel glared at his friend, "I'm still tempted to take her name off the list."

"Then why don't you?" Iris asked, curious.

Daniel found he didn't have an answer.

CHAPTER THREE

The paper-lined windows of the McInnis's Print Shop could stop people in their tracks. Almost every windowpane framed a drawing, etching, or caricature, each with its own story to tell. Stella surveyed the crowd gathered in front of the colourful windows. A part of her wanted to announce to the throng of people that the art they viewed was hers, but the part that valued her reputation and anonymity kept silent. Stella skirted around the crowd and into the haberdashery shop next door.

A bell tinkled as Stella and Laurette entered the store. Several ladies stood at the counter, with staff attending to their needs. One clerk looked up from where she was organizing ribbons. A grin lit her face as she recognized them. "Good day, Miss Denton, Miss Dubois."

"Good day, Patience."

"Come, let me show you your order." Patience set aside the box of ribbons and beckoned them to follow her through the back of the store. She brought them into the storage room. "I liked your most recent caricatures, madam. Especially the one of the arrogant aristocrat."

"Thank you." Stella's lips twitched into a grin. Patience was one of a handful of people who knew her identity. The girl led them from the back room into the alley behind the shop. Seeing that it was empty, Patience bid them good day before returning to her work.

It was the same routine every time. Stella knew there would be serious consequences if her identity as E. Starr was known. So she, the McInnises, and the owner of the haberdashery shop had come up with the plan to use the haberdashers as her access to the print shop.

Stella and Laurette crossed the narrow alley and stood at the unmarked door. Laurette knocked on the door, and both women stepped back in anticipation.

The door swung open, and the smell of fresh paper and ink wafted into the alley.

"Good afternoon, Mr. McInnis." Stella smiled.

The red-haired shopkeeper holding the door looked at the two women, his handsome face breaking into a grin. "Good afternoon, ladies."

He beckoned them to follow him and shut the door. A shiver of excitement ran down Stella's spine. She loved seeing her caricatures come to life. They wandered past a group of women meticulously adding colour and life to the black-and-white prints, many of them *her* prints. An apprentice in a leather apron sat at a large work table, working on the finishing touches of an etching. The man gave them a quick glance before returning to his delicate task.

Mr. McInnis led them into his office. The solid wood door muffled the noise from the workshop, allowing them to converse in a normal tone.

He motioned for the women to sit before settling into his chair. He eyed the portfolio in Stella's hand. "Well, Miss Denton, what have you made me this time?"

Stella set her leather portfolio on the large ink-stained desk in front of her. Mr. McInnis perched a pair of spectacles on his nose and removed the papers from within. He settled the pages gently onto the desk and surveyed them as a whole before picking them up one by one.

The silence filling the room as Mr. McInnis examined each caricature was broken only by the dulled sound of the press.

The caricatures comprised of several scenes and members of the ton based on the events she'd attended in the past week and what she'd read in the society pages. Debutantes being presented at the queen's drawing room in their ridiculous dresses, the actors on stage watching the theatregoers perform.

"I'll take these four," Mr. McInnis announced as he spread out the sketches out on his desk. He shuffled the other papers, returning them back into the portfolio. Stella grinned, pleased at the choices.

"That drawing you did of the arrogant aristo last week was one of my best-selling prints. I want more."

Stella straightened in her seat and struggled to keep a grin off her face. She'd thrown in the drawing into her portfolio on a whim. Generally, she made her caricatures vague. It kept people guessing and buying, but the Lord Beechingstoke drawing was too good to not share.

Her smiled dimmed. She must draw more of him, but Lord Beechingstoke was unpredictable in his movements, and he didn't necessarily attend the same events as Stella. He appeared to be avoiding events with debutantes like her.

Mr. McInnis leaned over in his chair, capturing Stella's attention. He pulled out a small book from a drawer. Flicking the pages, he picked up his quill and dipped it into ink. "Will the funds be going to the same place as always?"

"Yes, I'll be out at the Willows next week." She was fortunate that she had no personal need for the funds from the caricatures, so she instead used the funds to support the Willows, a charity she and Lady Redwick sponsored.

"Very well." Mr. McInnis made notations in the ledger and turned the book towards Stella. She reviewed the sum and added her initials next to his. "Mrs. McInnis sends her greetings. She's training a new clerk today and is unable to get away."

Stella's lips twitched at the pride in Mr. McInnis's voice. Mrs. McInnis managed the storefront while Mr. McInnis supervised the printing. It was Mrs. McInnis who had taken a chance on Stella's first drawings, and she had a place in Stella's heart for it. Mrs. McInnis was a shrewd business owner and a staunch supporter of women making their own way in the world.

Satisfied, Stella rose from her seat. She thanked the man and turned away, her mind already on the new caricatures she was planning in her head.

Daniel looked at the drawing and crumpled it in his fist, wishing the act could harm the artist as much as it harmed him. He tossed the offensive object into the fire, but the attacking flames did little to soothe the rage within him.

The image was another one of him; he was certain of it. There was no other way the gentleman in the caricature could be anyone but him.

It showed three giggling young ladies in a semi-circle. One of the ladies held a puppet of a man that all of the ladies were examining—a man who looked a lot like Daniel. The caption below read, *Entertained by the Earl. Which young ladies will become the puppet-master—or shall we say, puppet-mistress?*

He prowled the room like a caged wolf. What had he done to deserve being on the receiving end of Starr's ire?

The caricature brought back memories, bitter memories, of times he longed to forget. The image of his father and *that* woman, the one that he was supposed to know nothing about, and yet everyone else whispered about when they thought he couldn't hear.

He had been just a boy of twelve when he saw the caricature and understood what it was implying. It was a bitter pill to swallow, to realize that his parents' marriage was a sham, something to make sure money and power stayed between aristocratic families— nothing more, nothing less.

He remembered the image, the one his mother thought to hide from him. How could he forget? He'd come upon her in her sitting room, staring at the image before she crumpled it and tossed it into the unlit fireplace. His curiosity overtook him, and Daniel picked the image out of the fire after she left the room. He blew off the cold ash and smoothed it out on the floor in front of the fireplace.

He was confused at first; it was just a caricature. Why would his mother be upset at a silly drawing? Then he took a closer look. It was of a man and two women. One woman was dressed in finery and stood as elegantly as his own mother. The other woman was dressed like the ladies above the pub, the ones Daniel wasn't supposed to know about. The more scantily clad woman had two children at her feet, both crying and reaching for the man in the middle.

The man in the middle reminded Daniel of his father dressed for court. He stood closer to the scantily clad woman and sneered at the elegantly dressed woman.

Daniel read the caption, something he didn't understand. This wasn't like the images in his books; this was something more, something one needed to read between the lines to discover the message. Suddenly, like a tumble of a lock, everything clicked into place, and Daniel's world came crashing down.

He understood now why his father was gone for weeks on end and would then return, sullen and bitter. His parents rarely spoke, and when they did, there was a hostility, an ice between them that nothing could melt.

His father was happy to leave him and never happy to return. For years, Daniel thought it was his fault—if he had only been a better son, listened more, paid attention, did better in his studies, then perhaps his father would stay.

He shook off the bitter memories, crossed the room, and poured himself a brandy. Daniel swirled the contents of the glass before taking a sip.

There was no sense in dwelling on the past. His parents were gone. The family, the one that stole his father from him—the girls were just as innocent as him. He knew that now.

He'd met them once, at the reading of his father's will. It was the first and only time he'd seen his half-sisters, the children his father loved more than him. The late earl did one thing right, at least—he had left the girls respectable dowries, a legacy that would protect them financially. They had other concerns, of course; after all, they were born on the other side of the blanket, and illegitimacy was something that would never wash away. At least that money gave them a little respectability and protected them from the poorhouse.

Daniel knocked back the rest of his glass. He set it down with a thud, but refrained from pouring another drink. With any luck, this Mr. Starr's popularity would fade and Daniel could return to his relative obscurity in the ton and take this unwanted attention off himself.

CHAPTER FOUR

Stella was sure that the reason debutantes swooned was that ballrooms were overheated. This was the only conclusion she could draw as she stood with her back against the cool wall at the edge of the Woottons' ballroom.

It was an unseasonably warm night. The Woottons had foolishly invited everyone from the ton, and everyone had foolishly decided to attend. There were so many bodies packed into the ballroom that dancers had to manage the steps of the dances without bumping into people on the outskirts of the dance floor.

Stella opened her fan and waved it in hopes of finding relief. Instead, the scents of sweat, perfume, and cologne overwhelmed her, making her nauseous. She grimaced and snapped her fan shut. She elbowed her way through the crowd to the terrace doors and, once outside, gulped in the cool evening air.

The balcony was well lit, with a large enough crowd that she was confident that it was acceptable for her to be there without a chaperone. As long as she stayed in the light, she'd be safe.

Stella leaned forward on the balcony rail and peered out into the darkness of the gardens. Paper lanterns lined the pathways, making the back garden look either a like romantic paradise for a quiet meeting with a lover, or a path to ruin.

A breeze ruffled her hair. She closed her eyes, savouring the refreshing sensation, a welcome contrast to the stifling ballroom behind her.

The soft scuff of dance slippers on the stone steps caught her attention. She turned and blinked, just making out the shadows of a man leading a woman dressed in white to hurry down the stairs to the garden. Unease coiled in her belly. Even in the darkness, Stella could tell the young lady was not pleased to be led from the security of the terrace.

Stella glanced around, but no one was paying attention to her. She picked up her skirts and crossed to the stairs, descending before anyone noticed she was gone.

Away from the warmth of the ballroom and the safety of the terrace, the shadowy paths were darker, the breeze chilling. A warning.

She shivered as her vision adjusted to the darkness, taking a breath before heading deeper into the dark gardens.

A flitter of white caught her eye further along the

path. She focused on that beacon, ignoring a giggle off to her left, and a moan to the right. She would not lose the lady in white. Picking up her skirts, Stella rushed ahead with a grimace as her feet crossed the stones. Her dancing slippers were no match for the gravel path.

"Stop!"

The panicky feminine voice rang out in the dark, freezing Stella in her path. She heard a scuffle to her right, and she marched towards the sound. Around the corner, the dark shadow of a man almost enveloped the white dress.

"Come on, darling." A memory, unbidden, of a light, laughing woman flickered in her mind before she pushed the thought aside. She glanced around, hoping to find something to attack the man with. "We both know you want—"

A feminine grunt and the sound of flesh meeting flesh broke the man's speech.

He dropped to his knees, curled in on himself, looking more like a rock in the darkness than a man. She could just make out the lady's posture—fists clenched, ready to strike again.

"Are you all right?" Stella whispered. The lady jumped, stepping back, keeping her fists raised. Stella raised her hands in surrender. "I want to help."

The lady looked at Stella. "I will be well."

"Come. Let's get back before you're noticed." Stella walked around the man on the ground, pulling at her skirts, as if dodging a questionable substance. She clutched the lady by the arm and quickly walked away from the scene. They had to return to the terrace. There was safety in numbers and in the light.

Paying no heed to other couples in the shadows, they scurried back to the terrace, only catching their breaths in that space where the lights from the ballroom met the shadows of the back garden.

Stella surveyed the lady before reaching out and tucking a couple of loose hairpins back into her hair. "There. Now it only looks as though you've danced too much."

"Thank you." The lady sighed. "I appreciate your discretion."

"No one deserves to be caught in a compromising position." Stella shivered. Now was not the time to dwell on the past and those she couldn't save. "May I ask you a question?"

The lady bit her lip and nodded.

"Who taught you to bring him to his knees?"

A bubble of laughter escaped the lady's lips. "My... Harry. He insisted I know how to protect myself when he couldn't be there to protect me."

"He sounds wonderful."

"He's the love of my life..." Her voice broke. She cleared her throat and introduced herself. "I'm Miss Cassandra Ives."

"Miss Stella Denton, at your service."

They stood silently, side by side in the shadows of the terrace.

Stella ran her hands down her dress. "We ought to

return inside, Miss Ives, before we're missed. Shall we find some punch?"

They moved across the terrace towards the open doors. A shadow of a rigid matron emerged from the ballroom. Miss Ives stiffened and clutched Stella's hand as they stepped into the light. Catching sight of them, the figure crossed the terrace towards them.

"Cassandra, where have you been?" the matron snapped, stopping in front of them. "Where is Lord Patterson?"

"I haven't seen him, Mother." Miss Ives turned to Stella. "Neither of us has."

The lady gasped as she caught sight of them, her posture stiffening. Stella's heart plummeted. Was there something on Miss Ives's person that revealed her skirmish in the dark?

"Cassandra, what are you doing with *her*?"

Stella's brow furrowed as she looked from mother to daughter. A mixture of relief and confusion filled her. Why would the lady have such an antipathy towards her? What had she done to this stranger?

"Mother, may I present Miss Denton?" Miss Ives gestured from one woman to the other. "Miss Denton, my mother, Lady Sinclair."

Oh. Stella bit the inside of her cheek as she dipped into a curtsey. This was not good. Lady Sinclair and Stella's late mother had a falling out when they were debutantes. Stella's mother had died years ago, but evidently Lady Sinclair still held a grudge.

"I wasn't aware that the two of you knew one another." Lady Sinclair sniffed.

"It's a recent acquaintance, my lady." Stella smiled.

Miss Ives's sigh was imperceptible. "We'll be inside in a moment, Mother."

"Do hurry, Cassandra. Lord Beechingstoke has arrived. Go see if you can secure a dance with him."

"Very well, Mother." Miss Ives threaded her arm through Stella's. "We'll go find him."

CHAPTER FIVE

Daniel eyed the terrace with longing. It was a crush at the Woottons, and the overstuffed townhome was hot and malodorous. He pulled his timepiece from his pocket, wondering, not for the first time, when he could escape the party. His comfortable study and a glass of brandy were calling his name at home.

Thwack. Daniel grimaced as a fan smacked his arm. He shut his watch case and stuffed it into his pocket.

"Do you want every hostess up in arms against you?" Iris hissed. She had snuck up on him, which was impressive, considering she wore a bright pink gown with silk roses embroidered onto the hem and matching rose-coloured feathers jutting out of her coiffure.

Daniel eyed her fan warily.

"She has another in her reticule." Lord Redwick,

Iris's husband, smirked. "She's taken to carrying two fans after you broke her last one."

"You need to rein in your wife, Redwick. She's a menace." His teasing tone took any ire out of the comment.

"Ah, but she's allowed to bother you." Redwick gripped Iris's pink-gloved hand and planted a kiss on it. "It's in our marriage settlements."

Daniel snickered and shook his head.

Iris huffed and crossed her arms. "Boys, behave like the gentlemen society believes you to be."

"Of course, my love, but you like it better when I don't." Redwick waggled his brows, and Iris's blush matched her dress. Daniel strove to not roll his eyes. While it pleased him that his cousin made a love match, he didn't need to witness such displays of affection.

"Oh, Lord Beechingstoke." The irritating voice made Daniel's jaw twitch. A cloying floral scent filled his nostrils, and he struggled not to sneeze. "We've been looking all over for you."

"Lucky you," whispered Iris. Daniel glared at his cousin.

Lady Sinclair, owner of the sickly sweet perfume, opened her fan and smiled. Daniel smothered a cough as her fan pushed more of her fragrance his way. He bowed, backing up a step to escape her scent. "Good evening, my lady."

"We're so pleased to see you. I wasn't sure you'd be at the Woottons this evening." She waved her fan, almost knocking a passing debutante in the head. Why did ladies use fans as weapons? "My daughter is so looking forward to meeting you. My lords, Lady Redwick, may I present my daughter, Miss Ives?"

Miss Ives advanced and dipped into a curtsey like every other simpering debutante. But then she did something unexpected. She twisted and grasped the hand of the lady behind her, pulling her into the circle.

He straightened at the sight of Miss Denton, and the desire to leave disappeared. It was the first occasion he'd encountered her since the art exhibition, and he wanted to make amends. "Good evening, Miss Denton."

Lady Sinclair's eyes narrowed, a fierce scowl crossed her face. "I see you're familiar with... her."

Daniel's jaw twitched, and the inclination to protect the artist rose in his chest. Iris smoothly stepped towards her, taking the lady's free hand in hers. "Good evening, my dear! Why didn't you tell me you would be here when we were at tea yesterday? You remember my husband?"

"My apologies for not informing you, my lady." Miss Denton darted a glance at Lady Sinclair before refocusing on Iris. "I was so entertained by your children that this evening's entertainment slipped my mind. How do you do this evening, my lord?"

Redwick bowed over Miss Denton's hand, before offering Lady Sinclair and Miss Ives a brief nod.

A memory flashed in Daniel's mind. He pulled his focus from Miss Denton and back to the young debutante. "Do you know, Miss Ives, I just remembered the last time I saw you. You were high in a tree with the Duke of Tottenham's sons, refusing to listen to your governess. That was, what, ten years ago?"

Lady Sinclair turned a striking shade of purple while Miss Ives laughed. "Ah, of course, my lord. Fortunately, these days I find my feet are firmly planted on the ground, unless I'm riding."

"Have you seen much of the duke's sons? I remember you were close with Lord Henry?"

Miss Ives flushed a delicate pink, but her mother spoke. "My daughter has outgrown her childish antics and childhood playmates. She's an excellent rider, can manage a household, and her needlepoint is exquisite."

Miss Ives would be a perfect wife then, Lady Sinclair implied. Iris's list flashed in his mind, and he decided she was right to cross Miss Ives off of the list. An overbearing mother-in-law was not a point in a bride's favour.

Daniel's attention returned to Miss Denton. She stood between Iris and Miss Ives, her eyes sparkling with amusement. Before his mind caught up with his actions, he'd extended his hand. "May I have this dance, Miss Denton?"

His heart hammered in his throat as she blinked in surprise at his outstretched hand. Her eyes glanced back up at him through her long lashes, and Daniel's heart flipped in his chest. Damn organ, acting strange around the woman again.

She swallowed and placed her hand in his. "Of course, my lord."

Daniel glanced at the surrounding crowd and stifled a frown. When had so many people joined their group? "If you'll excuse us."

He ignored Iris's smug grin as he led Miss Denton to the dance floor. They lined up facing one another. The musicians took up their instruments and the strains of a cotillion.

He bowed, and a spark shot through his hand as he grasped hers through the movements of the dance. Her lips parted, and she broke into a grin. Her enthusiasm was contagious, and his cheeks lifted into a smile on their own accord.

The steps of the dance made it difficult for them to converse. At the first opportunity, he said. "Miss Denton, I must apologize for my remarks the other day." She arched a brow as he continued. "I did not mean to belittle your work."

The dance separated them before she could respond. Perhaps apologizing while dancing was not a good idea.

"I accept your apology."

Daniel stumbled, recovering before he could disgrace himself. He exhaled, relieved. "Thank you, Miss Denton. I will strive to show the utmost respect for your artwork should I ever have the honour to see it again."

CHAPTER SIX

The Redwicks' townhome was ablaze with lights. Swirls of excitement danced in Stella's stomach as she ascended the steps. Lady Redwick didn't entertain often, so to be invited to a dinner party at her home was a coup. Footmen took their hats and cloaks before the butler led the trio to the parlour. Thoughts about who would be present swirled through Stella's mind.

"Welcome, my lord, my lady, Miss Denton. We're pleased you could join us." Lady Redwick crossed the room, her arms outstretched in welcome.

Stella waited for her parents to greet Lady Redwick before she stepped forward and curtseyed. "Thank you, my lady, for the invitation."

"It was only a matter of time. Lord Lynd, Lady Lynd, Miss Denton is a valuable member of our charity at the Willows. Everyone loves her, and she is a welcome addition to our committee." Heat crept up

Stella's face. Lady Redwick wasn't one to praise at random. This was a high honour.

She watched as her father and her stepmother, Lavinia, exchanged glances. When she first informed them she was going to aid the home for unwed mothers, they'd balked. It had taken a week of negotiations and a visit to the home with Lavinia to ensure their permission.

"We're pleased to hear it." Her father's approval meant the world to her.

Lady Redwick tucked her arm into Stella's. "Now if you'll excuse us, there's something that I wanted to discuss with your daughter."

Lady Redwick led Stella across the room, introducing her to several of the guests present. It was an eclectic group. Members of parliament mixed with scholars and patronesses of the arts.

"We wanted to thank you for this." Lady Redwick motioned to a sketch on the wall.

Stella removed her arm from Lady Redwick's as she strode forward and smiled. It was a framed drawing she'd done of the three young Redwick children.

"You captured who they are," Lord Redwick added, wrapping his arm around his wife. "I hope you will do another when they're older."

"Of course," Stella replied, touched. The children had been so delightful to capture on that afternoon.

Stella shifted from one foot to the other as Lord Beechingstoke joined them. The man knew how to dress. His cravat was expertly arranged in a waterfall knot with a sapphire pin. She suspected there was no need to stuff his coat with padding.

"Good evening, Miss Denton." Lord Beechingstoke bowed as she curtseyed. He nodded to the sketch. "I assume this is your work? I'm impressed the brats stayed still for you."

The affection in his tone for the children took the ire out of her response. "Yes, my lord. And the children were manageable."

Lady Redwick laughed. "She promised them each a drawing of their favourite toy. It worked for Samuel and Georgiana, but Mimi didn't care."

Stella grinned at the memory. She'd drawn Lady Georgiana's dollies set up for tea and Samuel's toy soldiers in a mock battle with his bunny as the general. As Lady Mimi was under the age of two, it was simply a matter of observing her as she captured her likeness.

"Those drawings are in the nursery," Lord Redwick added to Lord Beechingstoke. "You'll be able to view them the next time you're here."

Something captured Lady Redwick's eye. She excused herself, and Stella watched as she placed her arm in Lord Beechingstoke's and led him away.

Stella turned back to Lord Redwick and inquired about his children. They spent some time in conversation before he too was called away.

She stood a moment by herself, surveying the room. Studying people allowed her to add more life to her caricatures.

A hand touched her arm, and Stella jumped. "Good evening, Miss Denton."

Stella looked from the gloved hand and up to its owner, a smile crossing her face. "Good evening, Miss Ives. I wasn't aware you would be here."

"I don't know how Mama secured an invitation, but here we are." Miss Ives laughed. She leaned closer, her voice near a whisper. "Mama wanted Lord Redwick to marry my older sister."

Stella smothered a laugh. "Oh dear." They looked across the room at Lady Sinclair. She stood by her husband, her nose in the air as they conversed with another couple.

"Indeed." Miss Ives glanced at the drawing and back at Stella. "I heard that this is one of your drawings. It's wonderful. Did you have a tutor?"

Stella had attended school for a couple of years, while Miss Ives was educated with her sisters at home. The question led to a conversation about art tutors, methods of drawing, and schools for young ladies.

Dinner was announced. Stella entered the dining room on the arm of Mr. Griffin. She beamed as he moved to collect her. She was a cousin of his late wife, Grace, and found he was a comfortable man to be around. He had excellent manners, and, unlike many of the men she'd met, he genuinely listened to what others had to say. She wasn't interested in him as a potential husband, knowing how well he had loved Grace, but with him as her dinner partner, Stella anticipated an enjoyable evening.

Lady Cecilia Montclair was a delightful dinner partner, but would she be a delightful wife?

She sat on Daniel's right. The tight black curls framing her face bounced as she laughed. Her lively brown eyes sparkled as they discussed the latest opera in Covent Garden. Lady Cecilia adored the opera, and to Daniel's surprise, she was familiar with the actual stories. He suspected she must be one of those rare ladies who attended to see the opera rather than simply to be seen in society.

Daniel couldn't help but notice her father, the Duke of Rudleigh, kept glancing towards them from his spot further at Iris's right. If the satisfied look on the duke's face was to be believed, then Daniel presumed the duke would be open to his suit.

As Lady Cecilia became distracted by Mr. Westham, a cordial gentleman on her other side, Daniel directed his attention to the partner on his left, Miss Denton.

She looked lovely this evening in a pale blue gown with a pearl necklace and ear bobs. A matching blue ribbon was woven through her russet hair. She spoke animatedly with Griffin, seated on her other side. As the courses progressed, Daniel noted with interest Miss Denton appeared more at ease with Griffin than she was with him.

Daniel struggled to think of something polite to say to the lady. They'd conversed about artwork in the parlour earlier, but he still felt a twinge of guilt at how he'd disparaged her artwork at the art exhibition.

Miss Denton's voice broke through his thoughts. *Blast*. Here he was trying to think of something to say to her, and he completely ignored her attempt at conversation.

He cleared his throat. "I beg your pardon?"

"I asked what you thought of Vauxhall," Miss Denton said, studying him. "Lady Redwick mentioned you were there recently. I have yet to attend. Is it lovely?"

He met her clear hazel eyes, surprised by the golden flecks in her irises. What other hidden beauty would he see?

"Yes," Daniel told her, struggling to regain control of his thoughts. Vauxhall. It had been a miserable experience. He'd attended with a group of acquaintances he hadn't seen in so long, and after that night, he'd remembered why he'd distanced himself from them. "It was delightful."

Actually, it was noisy and crowded, and one lady flirted outrageously with him in an attempt to drag him down one of the dark paths, despite her husband's presence. It had been horrible.

"Of course." She nodded stiffly, and Daniel realized that his brusque tone offended her. He frantically thought of something else to say when Lady Cecilia interrupted.

"My lord, have you seen the most recent caricature by Mr. Starr?"

Miss Denton perked up. Confused, Daniel felt his ire at someone taking away Miss Denton's attention. He wanted her full attention, even though he couldn't think of a thing to say.

"Which caricature was it, my lady?" Miss Denton asked.

Lady Cecilia took a sip of her wine before responding. "It was Mr. Starr's most recent one. The dandies that are all flowers in a garden."

Daniel cleared his throat, wondering how he could change the topic from the detestable caricatures.

"I don't know why you like such rubbish," he snapped. Heat rose as he felt the gaze of both women on him. He shifted in his seat.

"They're just silly little drawings, my lord. They don't harm anyone," Miss Denton replied, her tone soft, but her body radiating anger. "There is so much horror in the world. Do we not need something to laugh at?"

"Has someone has ever publicly ridiculed you?" Daniel asked her. "Have you had the likeness of yourself or a loved one shared for the world to see?"

She shook her head, "No, my lord. But I—"

"Then you, madam, don't know of what you speak."

Her grip tightened on her wine glass.

"Beechingstoke." Griffin's warning snapped him.

Daniel took a deep breath, willing his shoulders to relax. He looked to the bottom of the table. Iris raised a brow, both in concern and warning. He exhaled, forcing his ire out with his breath. It was not as though the ladies knew his history with caricatures. There was no need for him to be upset.

"Well, ladies, let's agree to disagree about caricatures. Now, have either of you been to Brighton?"

~

Stella settled the glass chimney of her Argand lamp over the wick. The brass lamp was a new design, with an elaborate bowl to hold the oil resting above the light. The light of the lamp was much more powerful than candlelight, allowing her to draw better at night.

She pulled her dressing gown tighter around herself, before picking up a wool shawl to wrap around her shoulders. There was a chill in the night air and her fire was low, but the light from her lamp was bright enough to illuminate her work without straining her eyesight.

Stella picked up her hair ribbon from the evening, weaving it through her fingers. The dinner itself was exquisite—Lady Redwick set an excellent table—but much of the company left much to be desired. To be fair, Mr. Griffin was a wonderful dinner partner, as always, but Lord Beechingstoke... She shifted in her seat and pulled out a piece of paper, compelled to draw him again.

She ignored the twinge of guilt as she sketched the man's features. She'd given McInnis another caricature of an aristocratic lord in the image of Lord Beechingstoke but had promised herself she'd never do another one of him. Shame welled in her throat. She'd been angry at the time after his insult of her work—had she waited, she'd never have drawn something so recognizable. There were plenty of caricatures that openly mocked people, but Stella had prided herself on creating generalized caricatures, ones where the people in them weren't recognizable, even if they had been based on real people. She'd broken her rule for that first sketch of Lord Beechingstoke in her fury, but vowed that she'd never do it again.

Finished, she held her sketch to the light. It was of Lord Beechingstoke, in profile, beside Lady Cecilia. A frisson of jealousy cracked at her heart. Stella shook her head in exasperation. Why she'd been jealous of Lady Cecilia was unfathomable. The lady was kind, considerate, and liked caricatures. Despite the latter quality, she'd make an excellent wife for Lord Beechingstoke.

But it didn't matter who married Lord Beechingstoke, did it?

She shoved that thought away. Determined not to think about marriage, Lord Beechingstoke, or Lady Cecilia, she pulled out another piece of paper. McInnis needed more caricatures, and Stella had more ideas.

She set her pencil to the paper, determined to capture the rest of the abysmal evening. The outlines of three men came to life. Two were arrogant dandies with stiff cravats, and more fobs than sense. The third was a rotund, wigged older gentleman whose bulbous nose competed with his moustache. To their right, a tall, skinny woman with buck teeth had her hands thrown up in exasperation.

She could finally smile at it now, but at the time Stella had been incensed. The men, in a heated debate over who wrote "I Wandered Lonely as a Cloud," refused to listen to Stella's insistence that it was Wordsworth instead of Coleridge.

They'd ignored her, as many men do. Well, they didn't ignore her drawings, at least not when she was E. Starr. As long as she had her caricatures, she had a way to be heard.

Too bad she had to pretend to be someone else to do it.

CHAPTER SEVEN

T
his was a bad idea.

It was fifteen steps from one end of the
drawing room to the other. Stella counted
her steps as she paced. Thirty. Sixty. Ninety. Twisting
the ribbons of her bonnet, Stella retraced her steps
from the window to the door to the landscape of Lynd
Manor and back again.

"You're going to wear a tread in the carpet."
Lavinia, head bent over the stitches of her needlework,
missed Stella's glare. The clock struck the hour. Both
ladies looked up at the ornate clock on the mantle as it
chimed five times.

Stella picked up the note and reread the bold,
masculine script. Lord Beechingstoke had sent a note
to her father, asking for permission to escort her on a
carriage ride through Hyde Park.

After their awkward discussions at the Redwicks'
dinner party, she was surprised he'd asked. She

believed that he was at odds with her, but upon reflection, he was much more agreeable during their brief conversation after dinner. To her amusement, she found she was looking forward to going on a carriage ride with him.

A knock sounded at the front door. Lavinia grasped Stella's arm before she could exit the room.

"It would not do to be too eager." Her stepmother's tone was soft in Stella's ear. Stella nodded and relaxed her posture, and they listened as Brown admitted a guest into the front hall. She needed to follow proper etiquette.

They retreated further into the room. Stella smoothed down her dress and cursed herself over the wrinkled bonnet ribbons. How many times had Laurette and Lavinia told her she needed to be more careful with her belongings?

Brown knocked on the door before entering. A single card lay on the silver tray in his hands. "The earl of Beechingstoke for Miss Denton."

"Thank you, Brown. She'll be down in a moment." Lavinia took the card and excused the butler.

Stella moved to follow before she was stopped. Again.

"He's waiting," Stella hissed. The door was still open, and if not careful, voices could echo down into the hall.

"Let him wait. A lady like you is worth waiting for." Lavinia stepped closer and pulled Stella's bonnet out of her hands. She placed the bonnet on Stella's head, tsking at the state of the ribbons. She held still while Lavinia tied a jaunty bow under her chin. Lavinia stepped back, surveying her handiwork, and nodded. "You look lovely."

"Thank you." Stella cleared her throat, unnerved.

As if reading her mind, Lavinia placed her hands on Stella's shoulders. Their eyes met. "Stella, dear, just listen to the man. I know you've had a rough start with his lordship, but trust me, he's a catch."

With that, Lavinia turned Stella and gave her a gentle shove towards the door.

Stella exited the room and lightly trailed her fingers along the bannister as she quietly descended the stairs.

Her walking shoes made little sound on the well maintained steps, allowing her to study Lord Beechingstoke without his awareness. His stark white cravat was elegantly done, a contrast from the navy of his coat. He held his beaver hat and tan gloves in one hand, his other hand on a timepiece attached to a fob on his waistcoat.

Stella's lips flattened. She hadn't kept him waiting that long.

"Here's your pelisse, miss." Laurette bustled into the entryway, Stella's golden pelisse in hand.

Lord Beechingstoke looked up, fumbling with his pocket watch before bowing. "My apologies, Miss Denton. I wasn't aware you'd come down."

"Good afternoon, my lord." Stella curtseyed after she'd planted her feet firmly on the ground. She turned to Laurette, allowing her lady's maid to help her into her coat. She took her gloves from Laurette and put them on. "Shall we be off?"

A footman opened the door, and they descended the steps. In front of the house stood a curricle with a set of smart pair of bay horses.

"What a fine pair. What are their names?"

"Autumn and Cinnamon." Lord Beechingstoke held out his hand to assist Stella. She placed her gloved fingers in his, surprised she could feel the heat from his hand through their gloves. She sat on the seat and adjusted her skirts as Lord Beechingstoke rounded the curricle and climbed in the other side.

"And your tiger?" she asked, as the young man handed his lordship the reins.

Lord Beechingstoke cast a glance at Stella before he answered, "That's Matthews."

Stella twisted in her seat and gave Matthews a smile. He bobbed his head just as Lord Beechingstoke snapped the reins and they took off.

It had been some time since Stella had been in an open carriage and even longer since she'd last been for a drive in Hyde Park at the fashionable hour. Lavinia preferred to meet people at their homes or other more indoor activities. Stella preferred to walk or ride in the park in the morning when it was quieter, allowing her more time to think rather than be among the fashionable crowds.

They passed through Mayfair, and Stella relaxed in her seat. Lord Beechingstoke was a skilled driver and navigated the streets with ease. Once they entered Hyde Park, they slowed, allowing the carriage to be swept up in the current of the ton during the fashionable hour.

"There are so many people."

Lord Beechingstoke cast a quizzical look at Stella. "Do you not come out at this hour regularly, Miss Denton?"

She shook her head. "No. I was here once or twice at the start of the season, but haven't been since. Are people always this slow?"

Lord Beechingstoke smiled. "Yes. Are you disappointed?"

"I withhold my judgment." Stella scanned the crowds, mentally berating herself for not thinking to come sooner. Her hands twitched, and she longed to pull out her sketchbook and pencil to make preliminary observations and sketches.

The weather was a perfect spring day. There were people everywhere. Carriages of all shapes and sizes lined the paths. Some pulled to the side to converse, while others stopped in the middle of the path, heedless of who they were blocking to greet one another. Men and women on horseback navigated between the carriages, greeting people as they went.

"Miss Denton!"

Stella turned as a large landau drove up beside them. Miss Ives sat in the carriage with her mother and two other young ladies Stella recognized. She grinned. "Good afternoon, Miss Ives, Lady Sinclair."

"Good afternoon, my lord. And Miss Denton," Lady Sinclair said, adding Stella as an afterthought.

Miss Ives performed introductions to the rest of their party, ladies she'd attended school with. They all appeared to be young, cheerful ladies, greeting Stella kindly and giggling at Lord Beechingstoke.

"I didn't expect to see you here, Miss Denton. You mentioned you didn't like afternoon rides," said Miss Ives. "Had I known, I would have insisted you join us."

Heat rose in Stella's cheeks as she felt all eyes on her. She shifted in her seat, wishing to draw attention away from herself.

"Evidently Miss Denton needed the right encouragement." Lord Beechingstoke's amused tone broke the silence. She smiled gratefully at him.

"I imagine it was easy for you to encourage her," one of Miss Ives's friends said as she batted her lashes. Stella bit her cheek to prevent a smile. Lady Sinclair sniffed, but whether it was from jealousy that it wasn't her daughter with the earl or the silly comment from the girl, Stella didn't know.

"A warm sunny afternoon, and to ride in such a carriage? Why, Lord Beechingstoke's offer was too good to resist." Stella's tone was light. The girls laughed.

Lord Beechingstoke tipped his head towards the Sinclairs' landau. "If you'll excuse us, ladies, we ought to drive on."

After Stella promised to call on Miss Ives in the

next day or two, Lord Beechingstoke moved away from the Sinclairs.

They met with several other acquaintances, and Stella felt the weight of even more eyes on her. She shifted in her seat, unaccustomed to the attention.

"Do you take many ladies on carriage rides, my lord?" she asked, no longer able to keep silent.

Lord Beechingstoke pursed his lips in thought before answering. "No, I don't think I have this year. I've been busy with other activities."

Ah, that explained the scrutiny. Was she ready for a courtship or marriage? Oh dear. She grasped at his last comment. "What other activities do you refer to?"

"I have the duties of the earldom, which takes up much of my time. I'm supporting Lord Redwick in the Lords, and I have some investments. I also fence and ride."

"Do you have an interest in the arts? Is that why you were at Lady Winslow's exhibition?"

He laughed. A warm sound that made something shift in Stella. "I made a promise to Lady Redwick to attend."

"Ah." Stella smiled in sympathy. "I understand. Your cousin is a formidable lady."

Lord Beechingstoke barked a laugh. "Indeed, she is. Although,"—he regarded her—"if I may say, Miss Denton, she was right about you."

"How so?"

She felt the whole weight of his gaze on her. "That you were someone to know."

CHAPTER EIGHT

"Smile, Beech," Iris whispered to him. "You don't want people to think you're only here because Miss Denton suggested you come."

They were at the Harringtons' house for an afternoon salon and literary circle. Lady Harrington proudly attempted to reinvent the salon in the art of the bluestocking salons of the previous decades. While not as popular as the salons of earlier eras, Lady Harrington's entertainments were thought-provoking and an amusing way to spend an afternoon.

Daniel smirked as they entered Lady Harrington's crowded drawing room. Iris was right, not that he'd ever tell her. She'd lord it over him like she did everything else. "Everyone knows you're the one who demanded my presence."

Iris exhaled, pressing her palm to her chest, and shook her head. "Well. Honestly, Beech, I'm hurt. You want to court the girl, and she's here somewhere. You ought to thank me." Iris lifted a hand and waved to a lady across the room. "Oh, there's Mrs. Edwards. I wanted to speak with her about our committee."

Iris removed her arm from Daniel's and disappeared into the crowd, leaving him alone. He swallowed and searched for a friendly face. Preferably one with sparking hazel eyes and a smile rivalled the sun. Where was Miss Denton?

"Oh, Lord Beechingstoke!"

Daniel cringed at the voice that did not belong to Miss Denton. A matron dressed in jonquil maneuvered her way through the crowds. There was no avoiding her. "Good afternoon, Lady Sinclair."

As Lady Sinclair closed in on him, he suddenly understood how a fox must feel as the hounds closed in. He stiffened and his gaze darted around the room, praying there was someone else he could speak with.

"Oh, we were not expecting to see you here." Lady Sinclair dipped into a curtsey. She gestured to her daughter behind her. "Cassandra was just talking about you."

"Mama!" Miss Ives cringed and shot Daniel an apologetic look.

It took Daniel a great effort to school his features into a polite façade. "Good afternoon, Miss Ives. Have you seen—"

"She was so pleased to hear you were to attend with your cousin." Lady Sinclair grasped her daughter's arm and pulled the girl closer. "She was curious about what your thoughts are on the newest edition of Mrs. Smith's *Elegiac Sonnets*, particularly the newer poems."

Daniel's brows furrowed as he regarded the eager mother and embarrassed daughter. He'd known the Sinclairs since he was a boy. In fact, Lord Sinclair had been very helpful when Daniel had taken control of the estates after his father's death. He owed a great deal to the family, but marriage? No, he did not want Miss Ives, and she, thankfully, did not seem to want him either.

How could he extract himself from them without the risk of being compromised by an eligible young lady? Where the devil was Iris?

"I haven't read the most recent edition of Mrs. Smith's work," Daniel said.

Lady Sinclair pressed her lips together in thought. "I'm sure the Harringtons' have a copy in their library. You must examine it. There was one poem in particular Cassandra was interested in, and you might be as well."

"Do you mean sonnet seventy, Mother?" Miss Ives's voice was deceptively innocent, but her wicked look suggested to Daniel the poem was not another about spring or flowers or birds.

"Of course. Now be a darling and go find the book. I'm sure the Harringtons won't mind you in the library."

The hairs on his nape stood as Lady Sinclair cast a look between her daughter and him. He wasn't a green lad. He knew the signs of a parson's trap when he saw them.

Miss Ives huffed and gritted her teeth into the semblance of a smile at her mother before she threaded her arm through his and pulled him away. He allowed her to lead him to the other end of the room, but he would not leave the safety of the public area with her.

"Fear not, my lord." Miss Ives's tone was so quiet Daniel had to strain to hear her. "I, unlike my mother, have no designs on you." She patted his arm affectionately.

Daniel sensed the truth in the statement, and unease unfurled in his belly. "Thank you for your honesty, Miss Ives."

She shrugged. "You're far too dour for my tastes."

Daniel stiffened. Dour? He wasn't sure if he ought to be offended or not.

Something caught her eye behind him. She broke into a smile and waved. "Miss Denton."

Daniel's heart jumped. He cleared his throat and twisted. Miss Denton, her lips curled into a smile, walked towards them. She glanced at Miss Ives and faltered as her eyes met his.

Daniel bowed. "Good afternoon, Miss Denton."

"Good afternoon, my lord, Miss Ives." She stood in front of them, her hands clasped at her waist. "I see Lady Redwick convinced you to attend." Her gaze darted. "Have you seen her?"

Daniel shook his head and offered a rueful grin. "She disappeared shortly after we arrived. Apparently, Mrs. Edwards holds more interest than I do."

Miss Denton perked up. "Mrs. Edwards? Wonderful! I know her ladyship was eager to speak with her."

Daniel cocked a brow at Miss Denton. How would she have known?

Miss Ives engaged Miss Denton in a conversation over the merits of Mrs. Smith's work, whether her books were better than her poetry, and if her publisher ought to have put newer sonnets in a new book instead of expanding on earlier editions. "Mama mentioned there's a copy in the Harringtons' library. Let us go." Miss Ives looked at Daniel. "Would you care to join us, my lord?"

There was safety in numbers—after all, two young ladies could not be compromised by one man—so Daniel agreed to escort them to the library.

A couple stood at a table as the trio entered. They glanced up briefly before returning to the book open before them on the table.

Miss Denton and Miss Ives both took separate sections of the library in search of the books. Daniel wandered over to the unlit fireplace and examined the landscape above the mantle.

The scraping of metal across the floor caught Daniel's attention. Miss Denton had moved a step stool into place in a secluded alcove hidden in the library. Sunlight illuminated her form as she stepped up to search one of the top shelves. Daniel shivered as she trailed her fingers along the shelf. Curiosity pulled him closer to her, and he joined her in the corner, out of the view of others. What prompted her to look up there?

Miss Denton grasped the shelf with one arm and stretched the other out. Her fingertips brushed but failed to grasp a book. Unease filled Daniel as he rushed towards her. She stretched out and—

Thunk. The stool flipped over behind Miss Denton. She gasped and stretched her hands towards the bookshelf, propelling herself forward.

Daniel reached out, catching her in his arms, barely avoiding knocking his head with her own.

"Are you all right?" He scrutinized her features and ran a hand through her soft hair, checking for any bumps or blood. Her luminous brown eyes met his. Her scent of rosewater, lavender, and something uniquely hers surrounded him.

The world around him ceased to exist.

Mine.

The thought ricocheted through his mind and settled into his heart. Without thinking, he pressed his mouth against hers. She tasted intoxicatingly of sunshine, honey, and cinnamon. With a groan, he lowered his hands to her waist and pulled her closer to him.

Her hands slid up from the front of his jacket and into his hair. His tongue teased apart her lips. She gasped as he pressed her up against the bookshelf. He pressed his hips to hers again, eliciting another gasp from her lips.

A sound muffled by his lust-driven haze pulled

Daniel from Miss Denton's lips. He took in her flushed skin, dream-filled eyes and swollen lips. His hand twitched at her waist. Unwilling to let her go, he settled with scattering kisses along her jaw and neckline.

The shattering of a glass, along with a shriek, broke the spell.

"Lord Beechingstoke!"

He flinched. Miss Denton's horrified gaze met his, and reality returned to them both. As one, they twisted. He heard, nay felt, Miss Denton's sharp intake of breath against his chest. Iris, Lady Harrington, Lady Sinclair, and another unfamiliar lady stared at them in horror.

"What on earth are you doing in my library?" Lady Harrington demanded.

"We were looking for Mrs. Smith's *Elegiac Sonnets*."

Daniel's esteem for Miss Denton rose with the calm of her voice. She was no wilting violet. She shifted, facing the ladies.

"Alone?"

"There was a couple in the corner. And Miss Ives..." Her voice trailed off. Heat rose in Daniel's cheeks. He was so focused on Miss Denton, he didn't realize Miss Ives or the couple had disappeared. His stomach plunged, and he felt like a cad. He'd been so caught up in kissing her regardless of who was around or of her reputation.

"Did you find it, Miss Denton? I had to find the

retiring..." Miss Ives's voice echoed from the door of the library and died as she took in the situation. "... room. Ah, Mother, I wasn't aware you were going to come to the library."

"Cassandra, we are going."

Daniel grasped Miss Denton's hand and gave it a reassuring squeeze. "My apologies, Lady Harrington. Miss Denton just made me the happiest of men, and we... uh..."

Iris squealed, her arms outstretched as she raced towards them. Daniel braced himself beside Miss Denton moments before Iris practically threw herself at them. Miss Denton shifted into Daniel's firm frame at the impact of Iris's embrace.

"I knew it!" Iris turned from Daniel and Miss Denton to the ladies. "I knew he'd make her an offer, but I didn't think he'd do it here. My lady, this is quite a coup."

"Well, I never..." sputtered Lady Harrington, clearly bewildered.

Iris gritted her teeth and hissed. "Smile, both of you, before your reputations are in tatters,"

"Cassandra!" Lady Sinclair's outraged voice echoed through the chamber as Miss Ives joined Daniel, Miss Denton, and Iris.

"Congratulations!" Miss Ives kissed them both on the cheek to show her support. "I'm so pleased for you both. We all are, aren't we, Mother?"

Lady Sinclair's fists clenched and unclenched at her sides. Daniel pressed a reassuring hand against

Miss Denton's back, uncertain as to what Lady Sinclair would say. No one would insult his... betrothed.

"Well, as unexpected as your engagement is, I'm thrilled you chose my salon to... er... announce your betrothal." Lady Harrington beamed, clearly ready to spread the gossip. "Now if you'll excuse me, I ought to return to my guests. Congratulations to you both."

She exited the room, and the others followed, including Miss Ives, who shot them a sympathetic look, leaving Daniel alone with Iris and Miss Denton.

"Well." Daniel grimaced under Iris's glare. "As pleased as I am, we should leave now so we can discuss this betrothal without people overhearing."

Iris took Miss Denton's arm and walked out, expecting Daniel to follow. Daniel rubbed the back of his neck and suddenly felt a pang of empathy for his cousin's children for the scolding they must receive, knowing he was about to experience his cousin's wrath.

CHAPTER NINE

"Lavinia!" exclaimed Stella. "What on earth are you doing?"

It was a position Stella never expected to find her proper stepmother in—standing outside her father's study, ear pressed up against the solid oak door leading into that room.

Something momentous was going on behind that door.

"Shh!" Lavinia hissed. "This door muffles everything. Lord Beechingstoke requested an audience with your father."

"Already?" Stella stepped back and wrapped her arms around her abdomen. Memories of the kiss in the Harringtons' library earlier in the day flashed unbidden in her mind. She'd done her best to forget about how his lips felt against hers, the heat of his hands on her waist, and the softness of his hair in her fingers. Her face burned, forcing Stella to look away.

The harshness of Lady Harrington's voice was the slap of reality she'd needed to realize she'd been compromised for. Mortification rose in Stella. Her father had known nothing of the compromise. She had planned to tell him that evening once he'd had his evening port.

Lavinia had agreed with that plan. After all, she was the one who'd brought Stella to the Harringtons' earlier and was responsible for Stella's chaperonage.

"Does Papa know about..." Stella swallowed, the words stuck in her throat.

Lavinia's features softened, and she stepped away from the door and gathered Stella in an embrace. Stella inhaled, drawing warmth and strength from her stepmother. Lavinia rubbed Stella's back. "There's nothing to worry about, my dear. Your father will be disappointed, but you've secured an excellent match."

"I didn't mean to," Stella confessed.

Lavinia's gaze searching Stella's face. "Did he force you? If he did, you do not have to marry him. We can take care of him..."

An involuntary smile escaped Stella before she could smother it as she imagined Lavinia, a woman who normally wouldn't hurt a fly, doing damage to Lord Beechingstoke. "No, I was just as swept up in the moment as he was."

Lavinia searched Stella's gaze before giving her a nod. "Very well."

The door to the study opened, and the ladies jumped and separated. Stella fidgeted, knowing that she shouldn't have been caught outside the door like a mischievous schoolchild.

Her father cleared his throat as he crossed his arms, regarding his daughter and wife. She smothered the urge to flee or to place her back against the wall, lest she be given a smacking on the bottom like she had as a child. She recognized the shadow behind her father as Lord Beechingstoke, but refused to take her eyes off of her father.

"Well, my girl." Papa cleared his throat. "Was there something you and your mother were going to tell me?"

She reached up to twist a loose strand of hair. "I planned on informing you after dinner." Her gaze darted to Lord Beechingstoke. "I supposed there's no need now."

Her father harrumphed. "Well, we have a discussion coming, my dear." He glared at Daniel. "Your young man already received his."

Stella wanted to protest that Lord Beechingstoke was not her young man, but swallowed as she realized that for all intents and purposes he now was. Hers.

Oh dear.

Papa stepped into the hall and offered his arm to his wife. "I've given my consent. Now I believe these two have a few things to settle."

Stella watched as her parents walked down the corridor. She turned back to Lord Beechingstoke. Heat rose in her cheeks as she remembered the last time they were left to themselves. She cleared her throat. "Shall we take a stroll through the garden, my lord?"

"Daniel." He corrected as he offered his arm. "If we're going to be married, you may call me Daniel, or Beech in public."

She took his arm. "Very well... Daniel. You may call me Stella."

They walked through one of the parlours and out a set of French doors. Large fluffy white clouds raced across the sky like errant sheep escaping their shepherds.

She led him to the middle of the garden where a small bench was protected from the wind by a trellis of climbing roses. She dropped his arm and wrapped her own around her waist. "I didn't think you would call so soon."

"My honour dictated that I call on your father immediately." He clasped his hands behind his back. "Besides, nothing smothers rumours more than ignoring them and proceeding as if we'd meant to do things all along. A betrothal announcement will be in tomorrow's papers. Your father and I believe having the banns read will be sufficient. A special license will only fan the flames for the gossips."

Stella tilted her head and examined her betrothed. "Do you really care that much about what others think of you?"

His jaw clenched, and he pulled his gaze from hers. He was silent a moment before he answered. "My family has a history of disreputable behaviour. The actions of my father and, more recently, my cousin almost ruined my family name." He hesitated, and

Stella wondered if he would trust her with the story. "My father... my parents... well, they didn't have a happy marriage. My father preferred to keep house with his mistress in town than be with my mother. He flaunted their relationship publicly. There were prints made about the scandal, and the boys at school thought it was fun to show the prints before they beat me..."

Stella's heart leapt into her throat. No wonder he hated caricatures. She could well imagine how horrible the prints would be, particularly as a weapon against a vulnerable boy.

"Daniel, I'm so sorry." And not just for his past, but for the prints she had made of him. She shut her eyes, a debate warring in her heart and mind—should she tell him about her work, or leave it be?

He paused his pacing and took one of her hands in his and raised it to his lips. "Stella, it's not like you're the one who made those drawings. You have nothing to apologize for."

Ice filled her veins. She swore to herself that she would take her identity as Mr. Starr to the grave before she told Daniel.

~

Who knew there would be so much involved in preparing for a marriage? Lavinia, to Stella's surprise, threw herself into the wedding preparations with a zeal that left Stella wondering what happened to her stepmother and who was the woman who was so enthusiastic about the wedding.

When asked whether her planning was perhaps too much, Lavinia took Stella's hands in hers and said, "We need everyone to forget about the circumstances of your betrothal and focus on how spectacular your wedding will be. We don't need the gossips thinking this is some quick marriage to smother scandal. And this is a celebration, my dear!"

Her father encouraged her to let Lavinia have her way, so Stella reluctantly surrendered her wedding to her stepmother.

Daniel was no help either. He told Stella he had no concerns about who planned the wedding, as long as he didn't need to.

"Lady Lynd has it all in hand," he reassured her during one of their rides in Hyde Park. She gave him a mock scowl, and he just laughed before gasping her hand and giving it a squeeze. "Everything will come together."

So apart from standing around being measured, poked, and prodded into articles for her trousseau, Stella had nothing to do with her wedding.

It was maddening.

And it gave her an idea. A way for her to create a story in caricatures that wouldn't damage her relationship with Daniel.

One afternoon, after being fitted for yet another gown, she stole away into her room and settled at her drawing board. Setting aside her most recent drawing of Daniel riding a horse, she allowed her mind wandered as she drew. It was a trick her drawing master taught her to allow her thoughts to flow from her mind and settle onto the page.

The figure of a woman emerged, tall and thin with a long aristocratic nose and square jaw. While not beautiful, the lady was handsome with a self-satisfied air.

Ideas formed as Stella filled the page with drawings of the lady. There was a mundane scene of the woman shopping with her mother and aunt, arguing over the cost of gloves. Another image of the lady surrounded by all manner of beaux from a dandy in an elaborate waistcoat to an old man stooped and holding an ear trumpet.

Her fingers flew across the page, and several more sketches followed as Stella fleshed out the idea. The images were more than a simple caricature. There were enough sketches to complete an entire book.

Brimming with excitement, Stella took notes, determined to go to Mr. McInnis with a concept as soon as possible.

CHAPTER TEN

The sun shone over the church of St. George Hanover Square. It was a rare sunny day, and Stella took it as a good omen. A few people were milling about in front of the church, but to her relief, it was not an immense crowd that she had seen at other weddings.

Stella exited the carriage and surveyed the large pillars. Taking a deep breath, she paused, the knowledge that she would enter this building with one name and leave with another threatening to overwhelm her. Of the names she was known by—Miss Stella Denton, Mr. E. Starr—the countess of Beechingstoke sounded so much more... daunting.

Cassandra, as Stella's last minute replacement bridesmaid, handed her a posy with a smile before entering the church.

Lavinia stepped forward to fuss and adjust Stella's wedding bonnet. "There. You look lovely."

"Thank you." Stella swallowed the lump in her throat. Lavinia had been her stepmother for several years, during which time the two had grown close. She'd miss her stepmother as much as she'd miss her father. Lavinia embraced her one last time before entering the church.

Her father cleared his throat. She looked up at him, a small smile softening his features. "Well, my dear, are you ready?"

"I suppose it's too late to back out now."

He narrowed his gaze, and Stella fought the urge to laugh. It was a joke in poor taste, considering the bit of scandal swirling around the way she and Beech—er, Daniel—were engaged. He'd given her leave to call him Daniel, and she needed to remember that.

Stella bit her lip, hesitating before she asked a question that had been in the back of her mind for much of the engagement. "Do you think Mama would have approved of him?"

Her father blinked, surprised at Stella's question. Since Lavinia had entered their lives, Stella and her father didn't speak of her mother often.

"She certainly wouldn't have approved of how your engagement came to be." Heat rose in Stella's cheeks; she'd never live down the compromise. "I suppose, yes, your mother would approve of Beechingstoke. She had a way of looking beyond how people presented themselves to the actual person."

Stella blinked the tears out of her vision and wrapped her hand around her father's arm. It was a touching thing for him to say, and for the first time that morning, calm washed over Stella.

"Now." Her father cleared his throat. "None of that. If I don't get you inside, Lavinia will come out and drag us in."

They shared a smile and entered the church.

As Stella's eyes adjusted to the darker church interior, she fought the urge to rub them. There were more people present than she expected. Lavinia sat with Stella's brother, down from Oxford for the occasion, and a few of their London-based relatives. Lady Redwick, who was determined to be called Iris, sat in her signature feathered hat and easy to spot in standing beside her husband and other members of Daniel's family and friends.

Cassandra and Mr. Griffin stood at the front of the church as attendants. She looked past them and caught her breath. Daniel stood tall and handsome in his elegant suit in front of the altar. This was it. She inhaled and took a step forward—towards her future.

~

I t was his wedding day.

A mixture of emotions filled him as he prepared for the day. He'd grown to like Stella, and he'd be happy to bed her, but he was still uncertain about his feelings for her. She would be a fair countess, an honest partner who wouldn't betray him, a good mother to any children. Yet he still felt like something was missing from their relationship. He shook off the negative feelings. It was just nerves, that was all.

He stood at the altar, with people dear to him sitting in the pews. Everyone was in place, except Stella. The door to the nave opened, but Daniel found he couldn't look back. As if sensing his agitation, Griffin whispered, "It's Lady Lynd."

That was promising. If her family were present, then certainly it meant Stella had arrived.

The first notes of the organ started, and Daniel straightened. It was time.

"Ah, there she is." Griffin said.

Daniel looked back, and his breath hitched as his eyes met Stella's.

Dressed in a primrose gown, with her hair pinned under a small bonnet, Stella walked towards him on her father's arm. The small posy of flowers she carried matched the silk flowers on her bonnet.

A slight smile touched his lips, and she gave him one in return. A sense of peace washed over him like a soothing balm, settling into place in his heart.

The minister's solemn and clear voice caught Daniel's attention as the service started. It was a blur of vows and promises spoken by both, and before he knew it, they'd promised to honour each other for the rest of their days.

Daniel slid a small square-cut emerald ring that had once belonged to his grandmother on to Stella's finger.

It was official. They were married.

The ink had barely dried in the register when he found himself alone with his wife in the carriage, scarcely knowing how they got there. His wife.

He studied her as she looked out the window, waving a hand at the crowd that gathered outside the church. To his amusement, her other hand clutched her posy in a death grip, as if losing it would be a disaster. She looked lovely. He wondered how long her hair was. His fingers twitched as he remembered how soft the curls at her nape were the first time he kissed her. Another part of him twitched, and Daniel pulled his gaze away from her enticing figure. They had a wedding breakfast to get through before they could be alone.

He grasped for something, anything, to say when Stella broke the silence. "Do you think there will be many people at the wedding breakfast?"

"I suppose we'll find out."

The carriage pulled up in front of the Lynd townhouse where the wedding breakfast would be hosted. Fresh flowers spilled out of the urns on either side of the front doors.

He took her trembling hand in his and assisted her from the carriage. Tucking her hand in the crook of his arm, he guided her into the house.

The butler and housekeeper stood in the entry to wish them both congratulations. Stella removed her bonnet, and Daniel suppressed the urge to turn and take her back to Beechingstoke House. Her tresses were piled on her head with two delicate matching combs holding the hair in place. He wondered what would happen if he removed the combs. Would her hair fall over her shoulders, or would he need to run his fingers through her hair to remove the pins?

"My lord, my lady?" The butler's quiet voice broke through Daniel's thoughts. He held his arm out to Stella, and they followed the man towards the back of the house. The doors swung open, and he announced with all the pomp and circumstance of the occasion, "The earl and countess of Beechingstoke."

A roar of applause thundered with a few piercing whistles breaking through the din. Daniel stood momentarily stunned at the people present. Good lord, did they invite everyone in the ton?

Stella faltered. He looked down at her pale countenance. A rush of protectiveness surged in him.

He leaned over and whispered into her ear, "Breathe."

Stella inhaled, her colour returning as she took another breath.

"There you are!" Iris greeted. She and her husband separated from the crowd. Iris leaned forward and kissed them both on the cheek. "Come, you must greet everyone before you can relax and enjoy your celebration."

"We should have eloped," Daniel grumbled to Stella and Iris. Iris laughed while Stella shook her head, a rueful smile on her face.

As they made their way around the room, Daniel was surprised and touched by the number of people present. The tension in Daniel's shoulders eased, and he allowed himself to relax and enjoy the breakfast.

"Congratulations, my lord, my lady!" Miss Ives crossed to join them, grinning. Stella's lips twitched into a smile, and she untangled her arm from Daniel's embracing the other lady.

"Thank you so much for standing up with us." Daniel grasped Miss Ives's hand and bowed. He had got to know her better over the past few weeks and enjoyed her company with Stella.

"I was honoured when Stella asked me." She grinned and asked Stella. "How is your cousin?"

"I've had word she's feeling better. While I'm sorry she got the measles, I'm glad you were able to fill in for her."

"She looked wonderful as a bridesmaid." Lady Sinclair added as she and her husband joined the group. "Not as beautiful as Lady Beechingstoke," the lady hastily added, "but no one can outshine a bride on her wedding day."

Stella's smile didn't quite reach her eyes. "Thank you, my lady. You're too kind."

Lord Sinclair clapped Daniel on the shoulder and offered his hand, distracting Daniel. Out of the corner of his eye, Daniel noticed Lady Sinclair's glare at Stella. He owed Iris, Daniel realized as he shook hands with the older man. Miss Ives was a pleasant woman, but her mother would have made any possible marriage between them a disaster.

"Ah, there you are! Aren't you going to introduce me?" a masculine voice drawled.

Daniel clenched his jaw. He looked into eyes that looked very much like his own. "I wasn't aware you were in town, Alton."

"I was curious about the charming lady who captured you." His cousin cocked a brow at Stella and winked. "Aren't you going to introduce us?"

He'd rather toss the bastard out on his arse, but he trusted Stella would see Alton for the man he was.

"We've already been introduced."

Both men looked at Stella in surprise. She narrowed her gaze at Alton. "My dear friend Miss Vincent introduced us at her home, Fanshaw Manor. You remember Miss Vincent, do you not?"

Alton frowned, then blanched as if remembering something unpalatable. "Of course. How is Miss Vincent?"

Her brows furrowed. "You didn't know? She passed away two years ago."

Alton stilled. Daniel narrowed his gaze as the other man swallowed. "That's unfortunate. My condolences."

She glared at him. "It was a complicated birth, and we lost both her and the babe."

Daniel's grip tightened around Stella's arm, and she leaned into him for comfort.

Alton took a step back and cleared his throat. "Well. If you'll excuse me, I have an appointment. My congratulations, my lord, my lady."

With that, Daniel watched as Alton disappeared into the crowd.

"Stella, what just happened?"

Stella blinked, as if fighting back tears. "My best friend was a victim of your cousin's *charms*."

Ire rose in Daniel, and he wished he could chase Alton and beat him to a pulp. Stella took a deep breath, drawing his attention back to her. "None of that. It's our wedding day, and Miss Vincent would never forgive me if we weren't to enjoy it."

He smiled softly at Stella. "Then, my dear, we shall enjoy our day."

CHAPTER ELEVEN

S tella prowled her new private sitting room. She pulled her new dressing gown tighter around her, wondering if she ought to have switched to her familiar, warmer robe. The pretty champagne silk was so soft and smooth against her skin, but it did nothing to keep her warm.

She'd dismissed Laurette, expecting Daniel at any moment. A quarter hour had passed with no sight of her new husband.

Husband. Stella took a breath, willing the butterflies in her stomach to still. She had a husband, and it was her wedding night.

She pushed away the thoughts of the night. Best not to think about what was to come.

The light of her candle caught the corner of a black walnut box. Stella sighed with relief and darted across the room, the candle's flame dancing and sputtering with the movement.

Her lap desk sat on a table in a corner. Laurette, bless her, must have ensured that Stella had the lap desk close by. Her larger desk for drawing had been moved into the schoolroom upstairs until it could find a proper place in her new home, but the lap desk would suffice.

She opened the desk and pulled out a paper and pencil. Stella settled into her chair and tapped the pencil on her lips.

An image formed in her mind. She set the pencil to paper and sketched. Gradually, the shadows of people standing in the church pews lined either side of the image. Flowers lined the aisles. In the middle of the image stood Daniel, watching her approach down the aisle. Her cheeks warmed as she reflected on that heated look he gave her as he took her hand in his.

She set the paper aside, determined to create another just like it in colour. The pencil failed to catch the glow of the stained-glass windows in the church or that his colour of his waistcoat perfectly complimented her gown.

Picking up another sheet, she smoothed the surface and started to sketch the wedding breakfast. Stella was determined to capture as much as she could from the day.

~

Daniel flipped open his pocket watch and checked the hour. He set the watch on his table, wondering if he'd given Stella enough time to prepare. Having dismissed his valet, Daniel stripped off his jacket, waistcoat, and trousers, draping the garments over a chair in his dressing room. He scrubbed his cheek. At this time of year, Daniel slept naked—should he don a nightshirt or just go to Stella as he was?

He pulled on a banyan and tied the belt. There. He was neither overdressed nor underdressed to see his wife.

His wife. Good lord, he needed to get used to that title. There was a new Lady Beechingstoke. He pushed away thoughts of the previous Lady Beechingstoke, his mother. There was no place for sorrow on his wedding night.

Daniel crossed to the door that adjoined both rooms. He paused and took a breath. Words of advice from Griffin and Redwick about brides and wedding nights echoed in his head. *Go slow. Be gentle. Determine what she likes.*

He knocked quietly before opening the door. Daniel took a step into the dark room lit only by the glowing coals of a banked fire, his eyes scanning for her. The room was empty.

Candle in hand, he walked towards the bed, just to be sure she wasn't hiding in the shadows. He turned around, puzzled. Where could she be?

The door to their sitting room was ajar. Daniel pushed it open, spotting his quarry. She was sitting at her desk, writing.

He entered the sitting room, taking in his surroundings. It wasn't a room he spent a lot of time in. He had some memories of his parents in this room, though none of them good. He and Stella would have to redecorate, Daniel decided, to banish the ghosts of his parents from these apartments.

The thick carpet muffled his steps as he crossed the room to his wife. The russet of her hair shone in waves down her back. She'd pushed back the sleeves of her dressing gown, exposing the smooth skin of her forearms.

He took a breath, inhaling her unique scent. He took another step. "What are you doing?"

She shrieked and whipped around to face him. "You startled me!"

"I'm sorry," Daniel replied with a grin. "I'll announce myself next time."

"It's all right. Sometimes when I'm drawing, I forget about the rest of the world." She exhaled, and he watched her body relax. He forced his gaze to meet her eyes, his pulse quickening. They were alone in the dark.

He nodded at the piece of paper she held. "May I see?"

She bit her lip, and lust shot through Daniel. What would her lips taste like this evening?

Patience. Go slow.

She reached for the page and was about to offer it to him when he scooped her into his arms.

She gasped and giggled, wrapping an arm around his shoulder for support.

"My room has more light," he offered as he crossed back towards his room. With a kick, he closed the door between the bedroom and sitting room.

Crossing the room, he lowered Stella onto his bed before snatching the paper and making his way towards the light of the fire.

His heart thumped as he examined the drawing. It was him at the altar, Griffin by his side. He glanced back at Stella, sitting on his bed, her arms wrapped around her knees. "This is very good."

"Thank you." Her response was soft. She looked so enchanting and vulnerable sitting in the middle of the bed.

He set the drawing on a table and stalked towards her. She scrambled onto her knees, reaching out to support herself with a bedpost at the foot of the bed.

Her beauty in the low light made him breathless. Daniel reached out, running an unsteady hand down her silk-covered arm and back up to her hair. He picked up a lock, marvelling at the various shades as he twirled it around his finger.

Bending his head, he covered her mouth with his. A wave of emotions for this woman washed through him. She tasted of mint and honey, overwhelming his senses. She slid her hand in the opening of his banyan and up his naked chest.

Daniel slid his hand over the flare of her hip. Grasping the soft fabric of her dressing gown, he pulled at the tie and pushed it off of her. He pulled away from her lips and, with trembling fingers, removed her night rail, assisting Stella in slipping her arms from the garment.

"You're so lovely," Daniel murmured as he surveyed Stella lit in the candlelight before him. Her eyes were bright, cheeks pink and lips swollen from his kisses.

He loosened his banyan and tossed it onto the floor. His eyes met hers. "Tell me if I should stop, and I will."

Stella swallowed and shyly nodded.

He kissed her again, parting her lips with his tongue, revelling in the sweet taste of her, and mingling his tongue with hers.

He urged her to lie on the bed and quickly followed her, revelling in the feel of her body pressed against his.

Wriggling against his lower body, Stella shifted closer. His cock hardened as she pressed her hips against him. She gasped, and Daniel pulled his mouth from hers, trailing a line of kisses down her neck.

Covering one of her breasts with his hand, Daniel gently massaging it, the pretty pink nipple tightening under his ministrations. Daniel bent his head and licked her nipple.

"Ooh!" Stella gasped.

Needing no further encouragement, Daniel

suckled on one nipple while his fingers played with the other. Stella writhed below him, seeking relief.

Rubbing her hands on his chest, Stella slid them below his navel and lightly gripped his cock. Daniel hissed, and Stella froze. "Am I hurting you?"

"No, no, it feels too good." Daniel shook his head and gritted his teeth in an attempt to slow himself. It was amazing to have her hand on him. He cupped her hand with his and showed her how to stroke him. To both his delight and frustration, Stella was a fast learner. He found he needed to break away before he spent himself on her belly.

Pulling out of her grip, Daniel laid Stella on her back again. Kneeling between her legs, Daniel ran his firm hands up along her thighs, parting them. He kissed his way up one of her inner thighs, drawing in a deep breath, inhaling her sweet, intoxicating scent.

She was wet, her curls glistening in the candlelight. Bending forward, Daniel licked her.

Stella gasped and rocked her hips against his mouth. Daniel kissed and sucked her while inserting a finger into her wet folds, and when she was ready, another finger joined the first. He looked up at the glorious sight of Stella, panting, hips writhing as she shattered, her inner muscles fluttering around his fingers.

Unable to bear it any further, Daniel lifted himself over her body and met her lips again as his cock teased her slick folds as his tongue mimicked the act he wished to do with her.

"Please, Stella," Daniel begged.

"Yes, Daniel," Stella moaned. Her eyes met his. "I trust you."

His heart fluttered at her sweet words. Kissing her again, Daniel entered her. Stella was wet and tight and felt so good around his cock. She whimpered, but he soothed her with kisses and sweet nothings. Gradually Daniel pushed further, filling her passage.

Withdrawing to the tip, Daniel locked eyes with Stella before slowly plunging into her again. Her gasp this time was not from pain, but from pleasure. He repeated the action, finding the rhythm that worked for them both. Stella whimpered and bucked her hips, seeking release.

Daniel held on as long as he could. He was so close but was determined that Stella find release first. He found her nub and rubbed his thumb against it as Stella whimpered.

"Let go, Stella," Daniel urged.

His plea barely left his mouth as Stella flew apart. With a gasp, she moaned, her hips rising, her inner muscles tightening around his cock. With a grunt, Daniel called out Stella's name and released himself into her.

Awareness was slow to return, as Daniel shifted, cautiously pulling out of Stella. Lying beside her, he wrapped his arms around her, leaning in to kiss her. Stella nuzzled in closer, boneless in his arms.

"Mmm," Stella mumbled. "We should do that again soon."

Daniel chuckled and kissed Stella on the hair, but she was already asleep. Shifting, Daniel blew out the candle before settling back under the covers.

Stella moved in closer to him, and he wrapped an arm around him.

For the first time in a long time, Daniel fell asleep, truly content.

CHAPTER TWELVE

"Oh, Stella!" Cassandra gasped as they climbed the stairs. "Are these the stairs to the attics? Should I be worried about you locking me up here forever?"

Stella laughed. "You read too many novels."

As they reached the landing, she crossed to the door of her studio, twisted, and lowered her voice into a menacing whisper. "Come and see my secret lair, my pretty."

She threw open the door. Cassandra clapped her hands and squealed in delight. "This certainly is not what I was expecting! It's so much better!"

Stella stood aside and watched from the doorway as Cassandra took in their surroundings. She fought the urge to wring her hands. It was the first time she'd had anyone other than staff up to her studio, and she was both anxious and eager to show off her work to her friend.

Cassandra picked up a paper and brought it over to the windows to better examine in the light. Stella frowned, not realizing that she'd left that image out. It was the first drawing of Daniel drawn shortly after their first confrontation, the one she'd deemed as too perfect for a caricature. His arrogance jumped off the page. She knew she ought to burn it, as it no longer captured the Daniel she knew, but could not destroy it just yet.

Cassandra laughed. "It captures Beechingstoke, the earl."

Stella liked that analogy, that the image was of Lord Beechingstoke and not Daniel, the man behind the title.

Setting the drawing back on a table, Cassandra picked up another drawing and gasped. Curious, Stella crossed over to her and examined the drawing. Her breath caught. It was a caricature, one of Stella's earlier ones, from before meeting Daniel. It was an image of a country girl holding a basket of tiny gentlemen, surrounded by well-dressed young ladies and their mothers. A banner reading "Marriage market—find your perfect gentleman" hung above them.

Cassandra looked up from the drawing. "Where did you get this?"

Stella took a breath, shifting from one foot to the other. "I drew that." She motioned to a pile on the table. "And those as well."

She watched Cassandra set down the drawing and pick up another. Wordlessly, Cassandra examined every piece of paper. Occasionally a smile crossed her otherwise impassive face. When she got to the last drawing, she smoothed it on top of the others, returning her focus to Stella.

"You're Mr. Starr." It was not a question.

Stella nodded, a weight lifting off of her shoulders. It felt good to tell someone else about her work.

Cassandra opened her mouth, closed it, only to open it again. "I'm speechless." She tapped the pages. "This is impressive."

Stella grinned and thanked her.

"Does Beechingstoke know?"

Stella's smile died on her lips, and she closed her eyes. "I don't want to tell him. He despises caricature artists. What would that do to our marriage?"

"And what would a secret like this do to it?" Cassandra countered. She gestured to the room. "He's going to find out someday. It's better to hear it sooner, and from you."

Stella swallowed. "Will you tell him?"

"No." Cassandra was emphatic. "Of course not. It's not my place. Your secret is safe with me."

Relief filled Stella. She reached out to squeeze Cassandra's hands. Releasing them, she picked up the caricatures and placed them inside the drawing board, under other artwork.

Closing the desk, she smoothed her hands down the front of her dress and regarded Cassandra. She smiled as an idea came to mind.

"Here," Stella said, motioning to Cassandra to the sofa. "I have a splendid idea for a sketch."

~

The problem with telling someone your secret was that sometimes they wanted to know more. Cassandra had begged Stella to take her to the printers'. She wanted to see how the caricatures were produced, and Stella reluctantly acquiesced.

Mr. McInnis's brows rose in surprise when, two weeks after her marriage, she appeared at his side door with Cassandra.

"Well, my lady, I thought you and his lordship would be on your honeymoon," Mr. McInnis said as he invited the ladies into his office. "And congratulations. When I suggested you draw more of the man, I didn't expect you to marry him."

Stella sheepishly grinned and cleared her throat. "I grew rather attached to him."

"You were certainly attached to him the day of your engagement," Cassandra said dryly.

Mr. McInnis barked a laugh before covering it with a cough. Stella took a breath, willing herself not to blush.

She cleared her throat. "We've decided to stay in town for the present." Turning to Cassandra, she made introductions. "Miss Ives, may I introduce Mr. McInnis? Mr. McInnis, this is Miss Ives, a dear friend."

"I forced her ladyship to bring me," Cassandra cheerfully confessed. "I've always admired your choice of prints, Mr. McInnis, and when Stella told me she was coming, I insisted on joining her."

Mr. McInnis bowed to Cassandra, clearly pleased with the praise of his shop, before he took the portfolio from Stella.

"These are rough sketches for a new idea I had," Stella explained.

He examined each of her drawings with a critical eye. For the first time, Stella was not anxious about his opinion of her work. Her confidence had grown as E. Starr grew in popularity, and she knew this idea was brilliant.

Cassandra's movements caught Stella's eye. She was looking at the copperplates spread out on a side table. Stella moved to join her.

The copperplate was one of the Prince Regent and his current chere-amie, a buxom, matronly woman dancing. The detailing etched into the copper was exquisite. Stella was envious. She wanted to try making her own prints in copper, but the steep learning curve and prohibitive costs forced Stella to leave the etching to the experts.

"This is how the prints are made?" Cassandra asked.

"Yes, the drawings are etched into the copper using fine tools and various chemicals and substances," Mr. McInnis explained. "One mistake can ruin the plate.

The deeper the etches, the more ink is absorbed, making that area darker."

"Fascinating," Cassandra responded with awe.

"It's delicate work, difficult on the eyes," Mr. McInnis added. He passed Stella the portfolio. "This is an interesting concept, my lady."

"One that will work well for us both."

Mr. McInnis stroked his beard. "I have to talk it over with the missus. We have to agree on something like this."

Stella nodded. It was one of the reasons she preferred the McInnises' shop, the partnership between the couple. Mr. McInnis might be the one in the workshop, but Mrs. McInnis was in charge of the storefront. She'd had to approve Stella's first few caricatures before Mr. McInnis could choose the rest.

Business attended to, Mr. McInnis escorted the ladies from the office and through the workshop.

Cassandra was agog at their surroundings. They stopped to watch one apprentice as he prepared a drawing for etching. With great care, the man gently and expertly applied his tool into the beeswaxed copperplate. A curl of copper rolled up from the plate as it created the etching.

"Come see Jem press one of your prints, my lady," Mr. McInnis said. Stella turned from the etcher and followed Mr. McInnis down the steep stairs.

A printing press stood in the middle of the room. It had a small iron cylinder sat on a flat table, with long wooden spokes shaped like a star poked out of one side.

The spokes were large, almost as tall as the man handling them.

The man, Jem, glanced up and tipped his forelock at them before returning to his work. He pulled an etching plate from the side table and dabbed ink into it.

"Jem needs to get the ink even across the plate so it sticks to the paper," Mr. McInnis told them. "He needs a light touch so the finer lines can be seen."

Once finished, Jem lined up the plate on the press. He then pulled out paper from a bath of sorts and used another device to wring out the excess liquid.

Setting the paper gently on top of the etching, Jem smoothed the paper and covered it with a few felt blankets.

"Miss Ives, would you like to help?" Mr. McInnis asked.

"Of course," replied Cassandra in a giddy tone.

Mr. McInnis led Cassandra towards the machine. Stella watched in amusement as both Cassandra and Jem pulled on the wooden handles of the machine. The motion set forth by the movement of the handles pushed the paper and etching through the machine.

Once on the other side, Jem removed the blankets. Then, with great care, he assisted Cassandra to peel back the paper.

"Oh, Mr. McInnis." Stella's breath caught in her throat as she saw one of her caricatures captured in the fresh ink. "I don't think I'll ever tire of seeing one of my drawings come to life."

Mr. McInnis chuckled.

Cassandra grinned at Stella, "Will you look at that! This is so exciting."

Stella's heart fill with pride, but her joy was not complete. There was something missing from this perfect scene. Or rather, someone.

She wished Daniel was beside her to share the moment. It was not a grand moment, but it was one full of joy that she wanted to share with him.

But it was not to be. He despised caricature artists. To tell him about this would ruin anything between them.

Stella turned away and pulled out her handkerchief. She really ought to get a hold of herself.

Taking a moment, she inhaled the ink and acids before returning to the group. If anyone thought something was amiss with Stella, they were too absorbed in their examination of the print to notice.

"Thank you, Mr. McInnis and Jem, for your demonstration," Cassandra said to them both.

"Yes, thank you," Stella added, now that her voice was steady. "We'll leave now so you can return to your work."

Stella and Cassandra returned to the coach. As it pulled away, Cassandra sighed happily. "That was so exciting. And Mother would have a fit if she thought I ever entered a print shop. It's a good thing she doesn't know!"

Stella nodded in agreement. Who knows what Lady Sinclair would do if she ever found out what they had been up to?

CHAPTER THIRTEEN

A thump and a giggle sounded from the nursery wing. What the devil was Stella doing up there? She'd mentioned that she'd taken over the schoolroom, but it was her house too, so he let her be. After all, it was a dreary place he'd always disliked as it reminded him of the worst parts of his childhood.

Daniel grasped the railing at the bottom of the steps to the nursery wing and squeezed. An idea flashed in his mind, stealing his breath. She certainly would've told him if she was with child. Wouldn't she? He shook his head. No, it was too soon for any such announcement.

Taking a deep breath, he forced himself to climb the steep steps. The carpet muffled his footsteps as he edged closer to the schoolroom. The sound of feminine laughter bounced into the hall. Daniel quickened his pace from the dark, empty hallway and towards the rich inviting sound of his wife's laughter.

Daniel swung the door open, astonished at the scene before him. Miss Ives lay on a settee, an elaborate turban complete with peacock feathers perched on her head and an old velvet curtain draped over her dress like an ancient Roman's toga.

Stella sat on a stool in front of a low easel. She wore a paint-splattered artist's smock. Tendrils of her hair hung loose on her neck. He couldn't see her face, but her laugh was as bright and cheery as the room.

Miss Ives spotted him first and sat up.

"Cassandra! I told you not to move!" Stella protested.

He crept behind Stella to surprise her and froze as he caught sight of the paper. It was a clever likeness of Miss Ives. On the page, the velvet curtain transformed into an elaborate and sumptuous gown. The settee, a Roman bench and a table of grapes set in front.

The Miss Ives in the painting had a mischievous and mysterious look, as if she had a secret joke that she wouldn't share with anyone else.

"That's impressive," Daniel said.

Stella squeaked as she startled and dropped the brush. He ignored the paint that had fallen onto his buffed boot as he picked up the brush, returning it to his wife.

Cheeks pink, she cleared her throat as she accepted the brush. "I wasn't expecting you home so early."

Daniel leaned to kiss her cheek. "Griffin had to

cancel. Is this what you and Miss Ives do when I'm not around?"

Miss Ives laughed as she unwrapped herself from the velvet. "Your wife is a talented artist, my lord. I've never had so much fun during a portrait sitting."

Daniel looked back at his wife, who was rearranging her brushes and studiously avoiding his gaze.

"If you'll excuse me, I'm sure Mother will wonder why I've been gone so long. I'll see myself out." With that, Miss Ives left Daniel alone with his wife.

They were silent and still for a moment. Neither wanted to be the first to start the conversation.

Daniel cleared his throat, "May I see your drawings?"

Stella glanced at him cautiously. "Really? You want to?"

"Yes. I like what you've done with that one of Miss Ives. I'd appreciate it if you showed me more."

She rewarded him with a bright smile. As she bustled into a corner, Daniel surveyed the room and the changes she'd wrought.

"The schoolroom looks a lot better than it did when I was a lad." With the addition of furniture, paintings, and lighting, she turned the cold, sterile schoolroom he once disliked into a warm and inviting art studio.

"Thank you." Stella's shy response was scarcely above a whisper.

He wandered over to the table she stood at, to better examine the portraits that laid in front of her.

Daniel picked up one of her father and stepmother and scrutinized it. She perfectly captured their personalities. Another portrait was a pencil sketch of Iris's brood, looking sweet and mischievous.

"That one I'm giving to the Redwicks once I'm finished."

Daniel pushed aside pages and picked up a sketch of himself. His heart sank as he reviewed the stern face staring back at him, the style oddly familiar. Was this how she viewed him?

Stella blushed and took the paper from him, setting it aside. "I drew that portrait the day we first met. I'm not happy with it. Can I draw you now?"

"Now?" He cocked a brow and looked down at himself. Was he presentable? Meeting her eager gaze, he sighed. "Of course."

"Wonderful!" Stella tugged his hand and pulled him over to the settee. Pushing him down, she took a step back, studying him.

She gestured to his cravat. "May I?"

Uncertain what she wanted to do, but amused and aroused by the idea of Stella taking charge, Daniel nodded.

She reached forward and untied the knot of his cravat. Her scent enveloped him as she unwound the strip of cloth with care. It was a shame she was wearing the smock, for it prevented him from enjoying a view of her bosom. Stella gathered up the fabric of the cravat and tossed it onto the floor behind her with a giggle. "I've always wondered if a man's head might fall off if I did that."

Daniel laughed, but it died as Stella stepped closer and ran her fingers through his hair. He closed his eyes and bit back a groan. What did he have to do to convince her to just make love with him on the settee instead?

Her hands left his hair, and Daniel felt bereft. Opening one eye, he found a flushed and pleased Stella looking at him. He reached out to put his hands on her hips, but the tips of his fingers scarcely brushed the fabric as she stepped out of reach.

He crossed one leg over the other for comfort and to hide his rising desire. Stella returned to her stool and prepared her materials. He fought the urge to squirm as she studied him with a fierce concentration. Then, without a word, she put her pencil to paper and drew.

The sounds of the scratching of her pencil on paper and their breathing were the only sounds in the room. Daniel feared to move a muscle, lest it make Stella frown.

At length, Stella set the drawing aside and returned to him. Daniel took a deep breath, then instantly regretted it as once again her unforgettable scent surrounded him.

She lowered herself so they were eye to eye. Daniel stared into those hazel orbs, wondering what she was about. She gave him a mischievous grin and leaned forward, whispering, "I missed you today."

She pressed her lips onto his in a gentle kiss. Savouring her taste, Daniel raised his hands and wove his fingers into her hair. He opened his mouth, his tongue teasing her lips.

Stella moaned, running her hands over his shoulders and down to where the soft linen of his shirt met his trousers. She snatched the hem and pulled it up so the shirt flew over his head, landing somewhere on the floor behind her.

He loosened her dress, allowing the bodice to sag, revealing her breasts. She leaned forward capturing his lips with hers and ran her fingers through his hair. Daniel slid his hand up her stockinged calf, caressing the delicate flesh at her knee. Her kiss transformed into a giggle as she set to kissing his jaw and neck.

He shivered as she ran her hands down his chest, her fingertips teasing his sensitive flesh. As she reached for his trousers, she hesitated, fumbling with the buttons.

He held his breath as she lowered his trousers. He shifted his hips, sliding himself free and adjusting Stella. Her touch was soft, tentative, as her fingers brushed his member—once, twice, before she took him in her hand.

He moaned and muttered words of encouragement as she adjusted her grip and pace. His hands slid further up her thighs, brushing aside the layers of clothing separating them. She kissed him again, tongues dancing as he slid a finger into the wetness between her thighs.

Stella whimpered and moved, wrapping one arm around his neck while bunching up her skirts with her free hand.

Daniel groaned as he adjusted her, the tip of his cock touched the wetness of her core, teasing them both. She gasped and lowered herself, enveloping him in her wet heat.

His hands grasped her hips, then shifted to cup her bottom. His lips captured hers as she slid down his cock.

He surrendered to Stella, allowing himself to be wrapped in her hair, her kisses, her body. He allowed her passions, their passions, to rise and crest before crashing into oblivion.

He lay on his back and leisurely traced Stella's spine as she reclined, boneless, on top of him. Pressing a gentle kiss against her lips he reached up to pull the velvet curtain over their bodies.

They lay there, in each other's arms, while shadows lengthened and crossed the room. A deep sense of peace filled him.

Daniel enjoyed Stella's fingers drawing circles along his bare chest. It felt luxurious to be skin to skin with his wife in the late afternoon sun.

Daniel regarded the room. Now sated, he had the time to see the changes she had made to the space. "How long have you been drawing up here?"

"A few weeks. You've been so busy, and I needed space to work."

"Work?"

Stella's breath caught. She hadn't meant to use the word "work." It slipped off her tongue, loosened by their lovemaking and the intimacy in the twilight.

"What sort of work?"

She studied him. He was curious, not upset.

Stella took a breath, deciding to peel back another layer from her secrets. "Sometimes I sell the portraits I make. It's not like I advertise, but word of mouth works well. I've had a few commissions from various ladies of the ton. I only draw ladies and children in their homes." This was true.

"So no one ever comes up here?"

"I've invited Cassandra up here, and Laurette and your senior staff know this is a studio. You're the only man I've had up here."

He relaxed and reached out for a lock of her hair, twirling it in his fingers.

"So my wife is in trade?" A trace of amusement lingered in his voice.

She laughed. "I suppose so. Will that be an issue?"

He was quiet for a moment. Stella stilled. As her husband, he could forbid her from drawing, and it would kill her if he chose to do so.

"No," Daniel said at length. Relief flow through her body. "As long as you don't repeat events like this with other men, I have no issue with your portraiture. It's not like you're drawing caricatures."

Stella froze. "Wh-what's wrong with caricatures?"

"They're nothing but drawn gossip. Caricatures can destroy peoples' lives."

"Daniel, you're exaggerating."

He shook his head, adamant. "Caricatures destroyed my parents' marriage and killed my mother." Daniel shifted, running his fingers through his hair. "I've avoided caricatures for the past fifteen years, and yet somehow I've ended up in them."

Stella swallowed, her stomach churning. "What do you mean?"

He sat beside her and took her hand in his. "Stella, there have been caricatures of me recently. Mr. Starr has drawn me in an unflattering light."

"Caricatures are meant to show people in a harsh light. Mr. Starr is a caricature artist, but he's not vicious," Stella reasoned. "But I meant, how did caricatures kill your mother?"

Daniel looked away.

Stella extended her hand, and he hesitated before he took it. She pulled him beside her and whispered, "Tell me."

He ran a hand through his hair. "I was at school when the first caricature was published. My mother had always known that father was unfaithful, but she hadn't known that he had a mistress and a family with her. The caricature showed him with his mistress and their daughters. I have three half-sisters I've never met.

"One of the boys at school brought the caricature in and taunted me with it. I threw a punch, but was outnumbered. That's how I got this, along with a black eye." Daniel twisted and gestured to the small scar on his right shoulder. She stretched out her fingers, running the tips along the marred skin on his otherwise flawless back.

"While I defended myself with my fists, my mother's only weapon was her words. She was in London at the time, so she experienced caricature after caricature of herself, my father and his mistress. I was told Father laughed at the caricatures and suggested to mother that she leave town, if she was upset." He paused. Stella's heart grew heavier with every word he spoke. "Between his mocking and open flaunting of his relationship with his mistress and the gossip, Mother couldn't bear it any more."

His voice cracked. "I got word at school. They told me she took ill and passed quickly. Two years later I found her journal. She wrote that she couldn't bear the silence, cold stares and insincerity."

He closed his eyes. Her blood ran cold.

"She killed herself. She drank too much laudanum."

He nestled his head against her shoulder as he finished. Stella closed her eyes, swallowing back the tears.

"Oh, Daniel." she whispered, her heart breaking for both the boy he once was and the man he now is. She could never reveal her secret identity to Daniel. Not after the damage wrought. To do so would irreparably destroy their relationship.

The revelation ate at Stella. The caricatures were a large part of her life, they gave her a way to express herself in a manner that made people stop and listen. On the other hand, she married Daniel, and he needed her in his life as his wife. Could she be both Lady Beechingstoke and Mr. E. Starr, or would she have to choose and crush a part of herself?

CHAPTER FOURTEEN

T he note appeared as innocuous as the rest of her post. Stella picked it up and flipped from the elegant handwriting on the front to the vaguely familiar seal on the back. She opened the letter and smoothed out the folds on to the black walnut surface of her delicate lady's desk in the morning room. A chill travelled down her spine as she read.

> Dear Lady Beechingstoke,
>   Or should I address this letter to Mr. E. Starr?
>   Yes, my lady, I am aware of your secret. To deny your identity as that detestable caricature artist is futile. I have proof in the form several reliable witnesses delivering copies of your horrible scribblings to the McInnis Print Shop, as well as several copies of receipts between yourself and Mr. McInnis. Even if you were to deny the evidence, you

are aware as I am that rumours are enough to destroy a reputation.

If you wish to have your secret kept from your husband, and the ton at large, please attend to me. If I do not hear from you within three days, I will go ahead and release my discoveries to the world.

She resisted the urge to crumple the paper and toss it across the room. Stella swallowed the curse words she yearned to shout. Her fingers itched for her pencil and a piece of paper to draw out her anger.

Lady Sinclair, of all people, had discovered she was Mr. E. Starr.

"Is everything all right?"

Stella jerked up her head. Daniel's gaze was full of concern. Her heart softened at the sight of him, then tightened again as she swallowed the lump in her throat. She longed to tell him, to unburden herself, but she knew he'd hate her and their marriage would be destroyed.

Oh, what a nightmare!

She calmly folded the paper and placed it at the bottom of her pile of post. "Of course. Why would it not be?"

Daniel walked towards her. It took every ounce of Stella's will to not shift the letter further into the pile.

Her breath caught in her throat as Daniel picked up an unopened invitation. She took a breath, willing her pulse to slow as he leaned against her desk and flipped over the invitation to the seal.

"You do realize that we don't need to attend every event."

Stella's gaze shot to his in confusion. "I thought you wanted us to be seen as much as possible."

Daniel dropped the invitation onto the desk. "We no longer need to be as concerned with appearances since we've been married for a month now." He pulled out her chair and gathered Stella into his arms. "Something's bothering you."

I'm one of those awful caricature artists, like the ones who tarnished the Beechingstoke name, drove your mother to her death, and a vicious woman is threatening to expose my secret. Stella tamped down the melancholy and fear that threatened to rise in her. She pasted on a smile. "I'm a little tired, Daniel. All the late nights are catching up with me."

"Perhaps you need to take a nap." He nuzzled her neck. "I think we both need a nap. Together."

Stella tilted her head to allow her husband to kiss his way to her collarbone. Her hands grasped his shoulders as he pulled her closer. Maybe they could retire. She could lose herself in him and forget all about the damned letter from Lady Sinclair threatening to destroy her marriage.

She flinched at the knock at the door. Daniel growled and lifted his head. He stepped back, adjusting her bodice, so she appeared more presentable.

"Enter," he called, his voice gruff.

"Begging your pardon, my lord." Simons stepped

into the room. "Mr. Griffin is here for your appointment."

Daniel cursed under his breath and dragged a hand through his hair.

Stella offered a small smile. "You better go."

"Please send for my horse and inform Mr. Griffin I'll be right there." As Simons left, Daniel leaned to kiss Stella's cheek. "I need to go." He pulled back, and his concern washing over Stella. "You'll be all right?"

She schooled her features into a serene smile. "Yes, I have correspondence to attend to."

He nodded, walked towards the door, then stopped. Stella held her breath as he turned, strode back to her, gathering her into a kiss.

"I look forward to our nap." He let her go and winked before walking out, closing the door behind him.

Stella wrapped her arms around her waist and shivered. With Daniel gone, a chill descended into the room.

A thought crossed her mind, and she rang for Laurette. She needed to go confront Lady Sinclair before the damage was done.

"T he countess of Beechingstoke," the butler announced as Stella entered the Sinclairs' parlour.

Lady Sinclair looked up from her needlework.

Stella crossed the room, dropping a piece of paper onto the table in front of the older woman. "Good afternoon, my lady. I received your note."

She ignored Stella as she pulled a blue thread up through the tambour in her hand. Stella stood, waiting to be acknowledged. When no acknowledgement was forthcoming, Stella sat, uninvited, on a sofa, spread her skirts and waited.

Lady Sinclair glanced up and sniffed with disdain. "One ought to wait to be offered a seat from one's hostess."

"It is the height of rudeness to not offer a seat to one's *betters*." Being a countess had its perks.

The look Lady Sinclair gave her would have caused a weaker woman to wilt. Stella was not in the mood to be pushed around.

"Your letter." Stella motioned at the offensive piece of paper. "How did you discover my identity?"

"So, you're admitting that you're that horrible caricature artist." Lady Sinclair set her embroidery on the table in front of her. "It was quite by accident, I assure you. My men are paid to follow Cassandra, who thinks she has more freedom than she does. You led them right into your secret. It didn't take much to steal into the print shop for some evidence."

Her heart dropped in her chest. She'd been so excited to share her secret with Cassandra that Stella had let her guard down and wasn't as observant of her surroundings that day. It would have been so easy for someone to follow them.

Lady Sinclair's eyes narrowed, and she lowered her voice. "You've brought shame to your family and mine."

Stella frowned. Ran her hands over her skirt, her thoughts racing. "I wasn't aware that we were related, my lady."

"You sketched my husband with that whore of a maid."

Stella raised a brow. "I don't draw specific people."

"You drew Beechingstoke. And you've drawn my husband."

Stella swallowed. That damn drawing she did of Daniel was coming back to haunt her. It was the only drawing she'd ever done where she'd made the person identifiable.

She smoothed out an invisible wrinkle on her dress. "Any likeness to someone dead or alive is purely coincidental."

"You lie!"

Stella flinched at the vehemence in Lady Sinclair's voice.

"You drew my husband with that... that horrible slut of a maid." Lady Sinclair hissed. "I don't know how you knew she was pregnant, but I will not have her shame laid at my family's door."

"My caricatures are never of specific people." Stella clenched her jaw, the pieces fitting into place. "If you see your husband as the villain, then perhaps you ought to protect all of the women under your roof."

One girl at the Willows, Molly, was a maid let go

by her employer once they discovered her pregnancy by the master. There were rumours about Lord Sinclair being handsy with his female staff. Stella swallowed. Between that and Cassandra's encounter with Lord Patterson at the Wootton's it was a wonder any woman was safe in Lady Sinclair's care.

"You need to stop drawing your hideous caricatures." Lady Sinclair demanded.

"Never," Stella replied without thinking. This might be the first time she'd received backlash about her work in person, but she would not let it stop her.

"You're just as selfish as your parents. Your mother's grasp in society was tenuous at best. The daughter of impoverished French nobles, no land or status to speak of. Your father was just as bad. He turned his back on duty and married the chit."

Stella's mind raced. Several conversations long forgotten about her parents surfaced. She gasped. "You were the one my father was to marry, weren't you?"

"He abandoned me for that French harlot." Lady Sinclair's eyes narrowed. "My father needed me to marry, one title was as good as another. Lord Sinclair was available."

She could not find it in her heart to pity Lady Sinclair. Not after being threatened with blackmail.

"That is in the past." Her ladyship waved a hand. "I'm certain your husband would like to know the identity of Mr. Starr."

The guilt of keeping the secret from him was already weighing on her. If she allowed someone else to tell him her secret, it could very well ruin their marriage. She swallowed. "What do you plan to do?"

Lady Sinclair picked up her embroidery, refusing to speak. Stella sat still, her hands clenched in her lap. She wanted nothing more than to plead with Lady Sinclair to not reveal her secret, but didn't want to give the other woman the satisfaction of breaking her.

At length Lady Sinclair looked up at Stella. "If you promise to never publish another caricature, then I won't say a word. Otherwise, I'll tell your husband within the week."

"And if I don't make that promise?"

"Then I will not only disclose your identity to your husband, but I'll tell the world what sort of creature you are."

CHAPTER FIFTEEN
THREE DAYS LATER

Daniel scanned the crowds gathered to see and be seen in Hyde Park. As they broke their fast that morning, Stella mentioned that she and Miss Ives planned to meet at the park in the afternoon. His engagements completed earlier than expected, and he wanted to surprise Stella.

A soft breeze kept the day from being overly hot. The weather was perfect, and it seemed like all of London was present for the fashionable hour. He weaved his way through the crowds, reminded of his first ride with Stella and how amazed she was at the number of people present. With today's crowds, he was grateful this time he was on foot.

An acquaintance he hadn't seen in ages caught him and stopped to catch up.

"Lord Beechingstoke!" a lady called out.

He excused himself from the man and looked up at the open carriage pulling alongside of him. "Good afternoon, Lady Sinclair. My wife informed me she and your daughter would be here this afternoon. Have you seen them?"

A flash of irritation crossed Lady Sinclair's face. Daniel regarded the lady. It might have been the bright sunlight, but something seemed... off.

"I have not seen them, my lord, but if you care to join me, we can look together."

He hesitated. While it was easier to move on foot, the vantage point of the carriage would allow for a better view of the park. Daniel climbed into the carriage, deciding that he could be set down when they discovered the ladies. He settled onto the bench across from Lady Sinclair, his back to the horses. The carriage began to slowly move through the crowds. He was silent as he searched for Stella and Miss Ives.

"How are you and Lady Beechingstoke faring?"

Daniel pulled his gaze from the crowds to the lady seated across from him. There was something in her tone that caught him off guard.

"We are well." A smile twitched at his lips as he remembered the intimacies from the previous evening. "We are settling into our new routines quite comfortably."

"I hope this does not offend, but it seems odd that you stayed in town instead of having a honeymoon. Most newlywed couples seem to go on a tour or to the seaside instead of remaining in town for the Season."

Daniel shrugged. "I have commitments here, and

my wife is content to stay in town. Besides, it's not safe to travel on the continent right now."

A shout of greetings distracted Daniel. Lady Sinclair shifted in her seat while he spoke, and Daniel wondered how he fast could excuse himself from her presence.

The carriage rolled on. Lady Sinclair opened the reticule on the seat beside her. She pulled out a piece of paper and held it out to him. "While I have you here, my lord, I wanted to show you something."

Unease coiled in his belly as Daniel reached forward and took the paper. He unfolded it. It was a caricature of a grey-haired man dressed in court finery, the seams of his jacket about to burst, his buttons quivering. He was laughing at an emaciated young woman, her cheeks hollowed with hunger, but belly swollen with child.

The printing below read *Why is one man allowed to fill his belly and hers while she starves?*

Daniel looked from the drawing to Lady Sinclair and back again. "It's just one of Mr. Starr's caricatures."

Lady Sinclair said nothing. She simply reached into her reticule and handed Daniel another piece of paper. This was a receipt between Mr. McInnis of McInnis's Print Shop and... he squinted, not certain his eyes were reading the signature right. *S. Denton.*

His jaw tightened. It had to be some sort of twisted joke. "I don't understand what you're trying to tell me.

You believe my wife sketched this caricature? My dear lady, have you taken leave of your senses?"

Lady Sinclair clucked her tongue. She pulled out a note, one from Stella to Miss Ives and handed it to him. He scanned the date, remembering when she wrote that note. The similarities between the signatures on the note and the receipt were too close to deny.

"I hate to be the one to tell you this, but your wife is a caricature artist. One, whom I may add"—she pulled out another drawing from her reticule—"is not above drawing you."

Dread filled Daniel's veins like ice on a winter's day. With stiff fingers, he took the drawing and fumbled to open it. It was the unflattering caricature of him sneering, done weeks ago... shortly after he'd met Stella.

His world tilted and shattered. Stella was a caricature artist, a successful one. He'd given her his name, his heart, and she could destroy him and his family name faster and more efficiently than Alton could ever do.

The urge to rip up the papers were strong. If it didn't exist, then the truth didn't exist either. He could go back to his happy life with Stella.

Or could he?

He narrowed his gaze at Lady Sinclair. "Why are you telling me this?"

The lady shifted in her seat and shrugged. "It is my Christian duty to inform you that your *wife*," she spat the word, "has the power to damage us all. And *you* have the power to prevent her from doing the damage."

The carriage slowed. Daniel glanced around him. He'd been so focused on his conversation with Lady Sinclair that he hadn't notice that they were at the gates of Hyde Park.

Daniel gathered up the three drawings. He folded them and stuffed them into his pocket. "If you'll excuse me, my lady, I must go."

He exited the carriage in a daze. Daniel turned away from the park. What had started out as a promising afternoon had just turned into a nightmare.

CHAPTER SIXTEEN

Stella paced in her sitting room, pausing by the mantle to examine the clock before resuming. They were going to be late to the soiree. She smoothed her favourite blue gown, one that made her feel beautiful and that she knew Daniel favoured. Pausing again by the clock, Stella distracted herself by examining her hair in the mirror, relieved to see the elegant new style held.

Daniel was due back hours ago. She checked the clock on the mantle again, rubbing her hands up and down her arms. She was full of worry and frustration. Stella had planned on telling him about the caricatures that evening, after the ball. It had been three days since her confrontation with Lady Sinclair, and she had been working up her courage all day to talk to him. It was not like him to be late without sending word. She refused to think something horrible happened to him.

Sounds from the corridor echoed into the sitting

room. Stella hastened towards the door. It swung open, and Daniel entered before she could reach it. He slammed the door shut.

Stella paused, looking from the door to Daniel, her brow wrinkled in confusion. He never slammed doors.

His eyes were never that icy either.

She swallowed the lump in her throat and straightened. "Are you well? Where have you been? I expected you hours ago."

"I had an interesting conversation with Lady Sinclair."

And just like that, her world shattered. She lowered herself to a chair and wrapped her arms around her waist. It had been three days. Three days! Lady Sinclair had told her she had a week to tell him. Stella closed her eyes. If she didn't keep her word on this, then what else would Lady Sinclair do?

She opened her eyes to the sound of rustling paper. Three pieces of paper laid on the table in front of her.

"When were you going to tell me?"

Stella swallowed, daring to meet his eyes. "Tonight, after the ball. I was going to take you up to my studio."

He paced, taking the same route she'd taken before his arrival.

Stella licked her dry lips. "I knew I ought to have told you before our marriage—"

"Yes, you should have. I'd never marry someone like you had I known what you are." The vehemence in his voice startled her. It was as sharp as if he'd raised his hand against her. He pointed to the drawings. "If it's discovered that you're the one behind these drawings, you could ruin our lives. I've spent years trying to bring respect to the Beechingstoke name, and with the stroke of a pen, you have the power to destroy it."

Her jaw dropped. "Daniel, who am I destroying? I don't target specific people—"

"Then what is that?" Daniel pointed at the drawing of him.

She blinked back the tears and wrapped herself in her anger. "That is just an arrogant lord. It's a caricature."

He picked up the next image, thrusting it towards her. "And this? You humiliated Lord Sinclair."

"I humiliated him?" Stella scoffed and straightened. "Lord Sinclair was not, in fact, the inspiration for *this* caricature. How can anyone be certain the image is that of Lord Sinclair? Enough gentlemen use their staff for their pleasure, tossing them aside once the girls are pregnant. It could have been any of them. Iris and I have worked hard to support women who suffer at the hands of so-called gentlemen. Men like him don't just deserve to humiliation, they deserve castration."

They stood silently facing each other, anger radiating in waves from them, both waiting to see who would make the next move.

Daniel pulled his gaze from hers. "Pack your things. I'm sending you off to Beechingstoke Manor on the morrow."

The pronouncement startled Stella. Her shoulders dropped as realization dawned. Daniel was serious about banishing her.

"I will not. Daniel, I—"

Daniel held up a hand to silence Stella's protest. He looked at her, his icy gaze that of a stranger. This man was not her husband. This was the earl. The frost in his voice was a stark contrast from the warm, sensual tones she was familiar with. "You may not have obeyed me before, but you will obey me now, Stella. You will retire to the countryside. You will not receive any callers, nor will you travel anywhere without my explicit permission, except to church."

A wave of anger rose in Stella. She straightened to her full height. If he wanted to play the betrayed earl, she could play the formidable countess. "Fine. I will rusticate at the manor, as you ordered."

She turned from Daniel, not wanting him to see her tears.

"One more thing." His tone sharp. "There will be no sketching at Beechingstoke Manor."

She whirled back to face him. "What?"

His face was impassive, "I forbid you to draw a single sketch, lest you cause more damage than you already have done."

Stella took a deep breath. He was the arrogant aristocrat of their first meeting again. "I knew I should never have married you. If you'll excuse me, I have packing to do."

She stormed off without looking back.

~

R age thrummed through Stella's veins. She tore into her room and kicked off her elegant slippers, sending them flying against the wall with a soft thud.

Finger by finger, she pulled off her gloves, crushing them into a ball, and tossed them onto her dressing table. Stella regarded herself in the mirror above the table, her face flushed with anger, eyes bright with unshed tears. Stella reached up and tore the pins out of her hair, tossing them onto the table.

They each bounced with a *ping* before settling in a pile.

"My lady?" Laurette's concerned voice called out from the dressing room. Stella heard the rustling of fabric as her maid entered the room. "Are you well? I thought you were gone."

"I am not going out tonight." *Ping.* A pin dropped to the table. A lock of hair slipped over her shoulder. "I will leave for the country tomorrow. His lordship's orders."

Ping.

Stunned silence filled the room.

"Very well, my lady." Laurette's voice was soft. "Allow me to help you."

Stella's hands stilled as Laurette pushed Stella by the shoulders into the chair at the dressing table. With a gentle squeeze on her shoulders, Laurette unclasped the necklace from Stella's neck and nestled it into the jewellery box.

A tear slipped onto Stella's cheek as she heard the click of the lid snap shut on the sapphire and pearl necklace.

A gift from Daniel.

Taking a shuddering breath, Stella closed her eyes, willing her heart to harden. Pins were removed from her hair and tangles brushed out, but Stella couldn't be bothered to care. Tears coursed down Stella's face as Laurette braided Stella's hair into a simple plait.

"Stand up, please, my lady."

She forced herself to stand and turned, allowing Laurette to remove the pins and tapes of the gown. Laurette efficiently removed the dress, petticoat, and stays. Normally this was the moment that Stella drew a deep breath, only tonight it was impossible. Every breath she took was tight, as if her stays were still hugging her body.

A warm, comfortable nightgown fluttered over Stella's head. As if she was again a child, she shoved her hands into the sleeves, before wrapping her arms around her body.

"Thank you, Laurette." Stella's words were soft, scarcely over a whisper. A smile of acknowledgement and pity flittered across Laurette's face, before her features returned to rest blankly.

Stella finished her ablutions before padding barefoot across the thick rug to her bed. Taking a deep breath, she pulled back the bedclothes and climbed in.

She sighed, grateful that Laurette had warmed the bed while Stella finished preparing for the evening. Stella pulled the bed clothes tighter around her, wondering if she'd sleep that night. The bed felt bigger, being the only person in it. Lonelier. She supposed she'd have to get used to it.

"Shall I pack? Or do you think his lordship will change his mind?" Laurette asked.

Stella placed a hand to her temples and closed her eyes. "He won't change his mind, but the packing can wait for the morning."

She lay in her bed, covers drawn up around her, tears streaming down her cheeks. Laurette had nestled the warming pan under the covers, but it was nothing like the heat Daniel gave off. Stella curled into a ball.

~

Dawn broke to a dull grey sky. Stella watched as cold light illuminated her room and everything within. She shifted on the window seat, adjusting her shawl to wrap it tighter around her. The shawl had been her mother's, and fingering the fringe brought back memories warm enough to keep the cool of the morning at bay.

Sleep eluded Stella. She tossed and turned all night, scarcely dozing until the harshness of Daniel's words ripped sleep from her grasp. Over and over she played their argument in her mind, followed by memories of their unconventional courtship and marriage.

She regarded the clock on the mantle as it struck seven. As the last tone from the bell died away, Laurette entered the room, pausing as she took in Stella seated, fully dressed, at the window seat.

"Good morning, my lady." Her maid's voice was cautious, polite, as if calculating Stella's emotions from her responses. "I wasn't expecting you to be awake."

Stella's mouth twisted into what she imagined was a smile. "Sleep proved elusive."

"Well, shall I order a cup of chocolate from the kitchens before I pack your trunks for the manor?"

"Yes to the chocolate, but there's no need to bring down the trunks."

Laurette paused. "Oh?"

She wasn't about to let Lady Sinclair win without a fight; she just needed some time to form a plan. And she certainly was not leaving London or her husband yet. "Pack enough clothing for a few nights for both of us. We're going to stay in town."

"In town?" Laurette's brows rose. "If I may be frank, my lady, your parents won't let you stay with them."

Stella drew a deep breath. "Lady Redwick will welcome me."

A grin lit Laurette's features. "Aye, my lady, I believe she would."

Together, Stella and Laurette packed the necessary items. After her chocolate, they prepared to leave.

"Is his lordship awake?" Stella's fingers trembled as she adjusted the ribbons of her bonnet into a neat bow. She wasn't ready to meet him this morning.

"Mr. Ernest said he's still abed." Laurette gently moved Stella's hands and adjusted the ribbons. She stepped back and nodded in satisfaction. "There."

Stella donned her gloves and picked up her reticule. Throwing back her shoulders, she took a breath. She strode out of the room, Laurette following in her wake.

Simons was in the entry hall as they descended the stairs. He stood at attention, surprised to see her up so early. "Good morning, my lady. I didn't expect you'd be ready to depart for hours yet."

"There's been a change of plans, Simons." Stella adjusted her gloves as she eyed the butler. "I'm leaving earlier than planned. I'll send someone for my trunks later."

Simons blinked and cleared his throat. "Very good, my lady."

Stella exited the house, and they walked down the street. A footman, Jamison, met them on the corner with a hackney waiting. He assisted her and Laurette into the vehicle before giving the driver instructions and hopping on.

The streets were quiet, as it was still unfashionably early. They passed several children with their nannies and various footmen dressed in livery running to and fro.

The hackney pulled up in front of their

destination. Jamison paid the driver and gathered their belongings while Laurette and Stella walked up the steps. Laurette grasped the knocker, the loud sound echoing in the quiet street.

The door opened, and the butler's brows rose in surprise before he moved aside to let them in.

"Good morning. I would like to speak with her ladyship, please." Stella offered her card and walked into the entry hall. Well, she'd made it this far. With any luck, this gamble would work.

The butler bowed. "I'll see if her ladyship is receiving, my lady."

They were left in the entryway. Stella tightly clasped her hands in front of her. It was that or wring her hands.

Footsteps sounded on the stairs. "Oh, my heavens. Stella, what are you doing here?"

"Oh, Iris." Stella bit her lip to prevent the tears from falling. "I've made a terrible mess of things."

CHAPTER SEVENTEEN

Iris was dressed in a pale pink morning gown. Her hair was gathered in a simple knot at the base of her neck, and, for once, not a feather in sight. Guilt rose in Stella's breast. She swallowed, aware that she'd taken Iris from her morning toilette.

"I'm so sorry, Iris. I didn't know where to go." Tears welled in her eyes, and Stella took a step back towards the door. "I can come back."

A gentle hand touched Stella's arm. "Stay."

Stella took a shuddering breath, undone by the kind tone. She allowed herself to be led upstairs into a sitting room she'd never entered. A work basket sat at one end of a sofa. Children's books were scattered across a table. Stella blinked and her cheeks reddened as realized that she was in Iris's private sitting room.

Iris pressed Stella onto the sofa and rang for a tray. Returning, she seated herself beside Stella. "Tell me everything."

And so she did.

Stella confessed to her confrontation with Daniel about the caricatures and his anger. His thoughts on the Willows. She left nothing out and held her breath, awaiting judgement. She wondered if coming to Iris had been a good idea or if she ought to face defeat and return home with her tail between her legs.

"Well." Iris leaned back on the sofa, her forehead creased in concentration. "Let me see if I understand this. You're Mr. Starr? *The* Mr. Starr, the caricature artist?"

Stella nodded and bit her lip. Had she done the right thing to confess her secret to Iris? She was Daniel's cousin, after all, and her loyalty would be to him first.

Iris leaned forward. Stella held her breath. This was a bad idea. Perhaps she ought to admit defeat—

Laughter broke through her thoughts as Iris threw her head back, unable to stay silent. Stella sat transfixed as Iris shook, tears of laughter streaming down her cheeks.

"You... you..." Iris gasped. She sucked in a breath and exhaled. "You're the one who drew Beech."

Stella bristled. "Not just him! I drew other scenes as well."

Iris grinned. "Oh, this is good."

"No, it's not! Lady Sinclair can use the drawings against the Beechingstoke name. Daniel's worked hard to return the name to respect."

Iris snorted and leaned to grasp Stella's hand.

"Beech is looking in the past. He is not his father, or his mother. Everyone knows that he's an honourable gentleman. He needs to look to the future, or he'll risk history repeating itself."

"He would never be so blatant or disrespectful as the late earl was." Stella objected.

Iris squeezed Stella's hand. "See, you have more fight in you than the late countess did. You and Daniel have really made a mess of things, but I trust that you'll both be able to figure it all out."

A watery giggle escaped Stella's lips. Making a mess of things was a gross understatement.

"And he wants to send you to Beechingstoke Manor?"

Stella nodded.

Iris settled back on the sofa in a most unladylike manner. "It's a drafty old pile of bricks. It's not in disrepair—Beech would never allow it to crumble into bits—but it's a gloomy old place."

Stella drew a breath, summoning the last of her courage. "May I stay with you for a few days?"

Iris tapped her lip in thought. Tension radiated through Stella's body. She could scarcely breathe, lest she missed whatever Iris said.

"Yes." Iris's voice was firm. She grinned, and Stella relaxed. "I believe my cousin needs to be reminded that women aren't to be sent to the country and forgotten every time he's upset. You may stay here for a few days. It'll allow you time to decide what you'll do next, particularly against Lady Sinclair. There ought to be a way to stop her from revealing your secret identity."

"Lord Redwick won't mind?"

Iris shrugged. "The man's so deep into his politics right now he'd likely not notice you were here. Besides..." She leaned forward and lowered her voice. "Don't let Redwick's pompous exterior fool you. He's a romantic at heart. If he's encouraging you and Beech to get back together, it's not because he's sick of you—"

"It's because I'm besotted with my wife and will do anything she asks, including sheltering a friend."

They looked across the room to see Lord Redwick, in his shirtsleeves, enter the room, Mimi in his arms. Mimi extended her arms and clapped. "Mama!"

Stella smiled as she watched Lord Redwick gently set his youngest on the floor so she could toddle across the room into her mother's embrace. Mimi gave Iris a kiss before snuggling into her arms.

Lord Redwick crossed the room and bent to kiss his wife's upturned lips. "She asked to see you when I popped up to the nursery." He stood and bowed to Stella. "Good morning, my lady."

"Good morning, my lord. I'm so sorry for intruding..."

He held up his hand and smiled. "It's no trouble, my lady. If I know anything about my wife, it's that she'll accept a friend at any time of the day."

"Beech was going to banish her to Beechingstoke Manor," Iris said as she focused her attention on her daughter. "Your uncle Beech is a fool."

Lord Redwick cocked an eyebrow and turned expectantly at Stella. She sighed, knowing as the man was housing her, she ought to tell the truth.

"It's nothing too scandalous," Stella said to reassure the man.

"She's the caricature artist Mr. Starr. Lady Sinclair discovered this secret, told Daniel, and is threatening to tell the world." Iris blurted out. Stella and Lord Redwick looked at her, and she shrugged. "May as well get it out of the way."

Lord Redwick lowered himself into a chair and leaned forward, observing Stella.

"You'd best start at the beginning."

CHAPTER EIGHTEEN

"**S**he's gone?"

Daniel's voice echoed in the empty corridors of the house. He ran a hand over his chin, the scratchy stubble reminding him he needed to shave.

The household was quiet, somber. A memory of the mourning period after his father's death flashed into his mind. Oh, how he despised that sad, heavy time. He regarded Ernest, his valet, standing quietly, awaiting instructions.

Daniel looked towards the door leading to the mistress' rooms. *Her rooms.* He'd slammed and locked the connecting door last night in a pique. For the first time since their marriage, he'd shut her out. But, he reasoned, she'd shut him out of a part of her life. That was unforgivable.

"I wasn't aware that she could pack that fast,"

Daniel mused, half to himself. "Which coach did she take?"

Ernest cleared his throat. Daniel turned back to the man, who was studiously looking at his feet.

"She didn't take one of the coaches, my lord." His valet looked up and swallowed. "She left on foot."

"On foot?" Daniel's stomach dropped. "Simons!" Daniel stormed out of the room bellowing the butler's name. Footsteps from a hall downstairs echoed as the butler came into view at the base of the steps.

"Yes, my lord?" Simons panted.

"What's this about my wife leaving on foot?" Daniel descended the stairs. "How could you let her leave? Where did she go?"

Simons's eyes were practically bulging out of their sockets. Daniel rarely lost his temper. "I wasn't aware that she needed to stay home until she left for the country. She left this morning with her maid. I assumed she wanted to go for a walk. It's not my place to ask, my lord."

A throat cleared down the hall. Daniel turned as a younger footman, one of the new hires, came cautiously forward. "Begging your pardon, my lord, but Jamison left with them."

"What?" Daniel and Simons asked simultaneously.

Simons frowned and shook his head. "I wasn't aware, my lord."

Tension in Daniel's shoulders eased. "When was this?"

"After nine this morning. I was looking out one of

the attic windows when I was gathering the trunks when I saw my lady and Miss Dubois get into a hackney with Jamison."

Daniel's jaw dropped. "A hackney?"

"Aye, my lord."

Simons cleared his throat. "Which direction did they go?"

"Towards Hyde Park."

Daniel frowned. What was his wife doing? She was supposed to be preparing to leave for the country, not jaunting around town, damn it. Would that woman ever listen?

"Very well." Daniel straightened, trying to ignore the worry building up inside him. "Send word when her ladyship returns. In the meantime, have someone pack up her belongings for her trip to Beechingstoke Manor."

~

Two days later

The thwip of the foil as it flew through the air, hitting its target, was one of the few things that satisfied Daniel at the moment. He altered his position, blocking Griffin's attack before ducking and maneuvering his sword to score another point against Griffin.

"Touché." Griffin responded by adjusting his stance and sliding past Daniel's defences.

It was a close match, allowing Daniel to escape from his troubles and solely focus on the movements.

"I have news of your wife," Griffin said, as he blocked Daniel's foil. Daniel faltered for a moment, then his wild movement in response allowed Griffin to easily dodge him and score another point.

"Do not discuss that woman here," Daniel growled.

"Fin!" the fencing master announced, clapping his hand.

Daniel and Griffin paused, both panting as they faced one another.

"My lord, you've had enough," the man kindly ordered. "I suggest you take a break, take this discussion elsewhere, and don't come back tomorrow."

Daniel nodded his thanks at the fencing master. He traded his foil for a towel from an attendant and wiped the sweat from his face.

"It's time we talk," Griffin said.

Daniel sighed. It had been two days since Stella departed.

His heart ached at the thought of his wife, anger and despair warring within him. He did not realize how much her betrayal hurt and how much he missed her until she was gone.

By agreement, the gentlemen made their way to Daniel's house. He poured brandy for them both as they sat in his study.

"Hard to believe it's been only a few days since your wife left," Griffin said.

Daniel knocked back his brandy, scarcely feeling

the warmth as the liquid trickled down his throat. He set his glass on the table. "I was a fool."

"You still are."

Daniel regarded his friend, "Did you know she was Mr. Starr?"

Griffin, who'd been sipping on his brandy, coughed and gasped. "I beg your pardon?"

"She's that bloody caricature artist, Mr. Starr." Daniel gritted his teeth. He wasn't sure now what was worse, the idea of her creating the caricatures or that she kept the caricatures a secret from him after their marriage.

Griffin shook his head and whistled. "You sure know how to pick a wife."

"You're the one who put her on that damned list." Daniel ran his fingers through his hair. He straightened and gestured at the drawings, paintings and other images spread across the floor. "She played me for a fool. She didn't bother to tell me about this. All my hard work to bring my family's reputation back to its glory, ruined by some scribbles in ink."

He watched as Griffin gingerly placed the papers back onto the floor and cross to crouch eye to eye with Daniel. "Did you even allow her a chance to tell you?" Griffin asked. His voice was quiet. Calm.

Daniel averted his gaze, heat raising in his cheeks. Their compromise probably made Stella more hesitant to confide in him. What would he have done, had he known about her caricatures before their marriage? End their courtship? Abandon her?

Shame rose in Daniel, and he took a breath. He knew with certainty that had he known about the caricatures, he would have done everything in his power to distance himself from Stella.

And what a fool he'd have been if he'd succeeded. He would have missed one of the best things to ever happen to him.

"She kept this from me, Griffin." Daniel eyed his friend. "How could she keep such a big part of herself from me?"

Silence filled the room. There was no need for Griffin to speak what Daniel already knew the answer to. From the very beginning he'd been drawn to her, as much as he was drawn to her art, albeit her drawings, not her caricatures. Still, she was an artist, a talented one at that. His focus on reputation and the damage he believed caricatures did to his family must have ate at her. How long could their marriage have survived if she was forced to keep such an integral part of herself a secret from him?

Griffin set down his glass of brandy with slow deliberation. Daniel felt the full weight of his friend's gaze. It was uncomfortable. "Have you looked through her ladyship's studio?"

"Why would I want to go up there?"

Griffin stood and crossed to Daniel. He patted him on the arm. "Go up into her lair. I suspect you will find something you didn't expect." He walked to the door, but paused before exiting. "And Beech, I'm certain there's a way to prevent her from destroying the

Beechingstoke name, if you just stop and think clearly."

Daniel sat in his study, watching the fire die down in the fireplace. Memories of his relationship with Stella floated through his mind.

He had avoided the studio since she left, but Griffin was right: it was time to enter her domain.

The house was quiet, and he hated it. She'd brought the house back to life and took that life with her when she left.

The studio was dark, but Stella kept several lamps, including her Argand lamp, in the space to allow for more light in the evening. Daniel lit them, then examined the room, forbidding his gaze from landing on the sofa and the memories it held.

He walked over to her oversized desk, running his hand over the smooth surface. What had she called it, a drawing table? Whatever it was called, it was a lovely piece of craftsmanship. He lifted the lid to the desk and pulled out a folder.

He opened the folder and jerked back as its contents scattered across the floor. He inhaled sharply as he examined an image. His mind immediately recognized it as a drawing from the Redwicks' dinner party. The man staring back at him had his own eyes and was obviously pompous, rude, and arrogant. He picked up another of him in his curricle, dated days before their marriage. It was unnerving to see the different portraits and how she'd captured his different moods.

His hand stilled as he caught sight of one she'd drawn of him on the couch in the studio. He was asleep, his hair mussed, chest and feet bare, the rest of his body covered by a blanket. Daniel leaned forward to see the tiny writing in the corner.

My husband, my love.

His breath caught. She'd never uttered the word love to him, and yet, here as he set the images into chronological order, everything fell into place. Here in front of him was a timeline of her falling in love with him.

His knees buckled as he sank to the ground in sorrow and awe. Confusion filled him. Here was undeniable proof that Stella loved him, and he had banished her from his presence.

Daniel picked up the scattered drawings, placing them back in the folder. Scanning the floor, he spotted a loose page half hidden under a chair. He scooped up the image, determined to add it to the others, then stilled. The image was an unfinished sketch, something he'd never seen, and yet was stylistically familiar.

It was a drawing of a young lady. She wore a pronounced and ridiculous hat on her head that obscured her face. Her companion, a gentleman, wore an excessively elaborate cravat and enough fobs on his elaborate waistcoat that it sagged under the weight. They were at the Royal Menagerie, where both the animals and other people stared at them, the words *"Who is on exhibit?"* scrawled above the image.

He replayed their argument in his mind, and what

Lady Sinclair had said. Griffin was right. Damn it, Stella would not intentionally destroy the Beechingstoke name. They could stop her ladyship from outing Stella as a caricature artist. There had to be a way. And what did it matter what she did with her work? She was a brilliant caricature artist who brought entertainment to so many people. While he didn't want to be one of her subjects, he appreciated that whatever she'd done, she hadn't done maliciously, or to destroy his good name. Their name.

Sickening thoughts rose in his chest as Daniel realized how much he hurt Stella. How could he fix things? Was he too late?

CHAPTER NINETEEN

S treaks of the late morning sun danced across the art studio, caressing the various pieces of artwork spread across the floor.

Footsteps tapped on the stairs. He looked up, bleary-eyed, at the shadow in the doorway.

Griffin gave a low whistle. "Did your valet abandon you?"

"Go away. I'm not at home," Daniel growled.

Griffin took a cautious step into the room, mindful of the drawings. "Yes, well, Simons knows you're always home for me."

Daniel slumped forward, muttering a curse under his breath about interfering staff. He just wanted to be left alone. Damn it, was that too much to ask?

He raised his head at the sound of rustling paper. Griffin had leaned over to pick up a few pieces of pieces of work to further examine.

"Lady Sinclair was the one who told me about Stella's work, did you know that?"

Griffin arched a brow in surprise. "I did not. How did she discover her ladyship's secret? And for what purpose?"

Daniel shrugged. Those questions had been gnawing at him for hours. He knew Lady Sinclair was not acting as a good Samaritan when she informed him of Stella's secret.

"Revenge?" he suggested. Griffin jerked his head up as Daniel continued, shoulders slumped. "Only I haven't any idea as to why."

Griffin shifted. "The list."

"What list?"

"Your foolish bride list. Well, Miss Ives was on the list, wasn't she?"

Daniel struggled to recall all the names on the list. Stella's was the only one that mattered. There was no need to think about anyone else.

"Lady Redwick struck Miss Ives of the list because of her mother." Griffin reminded Daniel. "Something about overbearing mothers-in-law."

Daniel nodded, remembering that conversation. "What of it?"

"Well. Lord Sinclair was a mentor for you, was he not? What if Lady Sinclair had designs on you for her daughter? By you choosing your own Lady Beechingstoke, and in such a manner—"

Daniel narrowed his eyes. Griffin did not need to bring up the compromise.

Griffin cleared his throat. "Well, she's bound to be upset. Perhaps she followed your wife and uncovered her secrets. Your wife and Miss Ives have become good friends, it's just a matter of time before..."

It seemed farfetched to Daniel. "What does she get out of it?"

"Petty revenge?" Griffin shrugged. "You're unhappy, and your wife is banished."

It had worked. It disgusted Daniel that he fell into the trap of a bitter woman.

He surveyed the surrounding papers. He reached out to pick up a folder and opened it. More caricatures, ones that hadn't been published, many of them had characters bearing his likeness.

An idea came to mind. It was foolish and might not work, but if it did, it just might be a way to remove any power from Lady Sinclair and to get Stella back.

CHAPTER TWENTY

Daniel had walked past McInnis's Print Shop before, but he had always avoided it and other print shops. Now he stood in front of the store, scanning the prints in the windowpanes for evidence of his wife's handiwork.

He spotted several, and while they didn't quite fill him with pride, it pleased him to see that her work was much admired.

The door opened, and a customer exited. Daniel took a deep breath and stepped into the print shop. The scent of ink and paper assailed him. Several customers lingered, browsed with a handful of shop clerks assisting them. Daniel caught the eye of a willowy, brown-skinned shopkeeper in an apron and cap. She smiled at him in greeting. "How may I help you, sir?"

Daniel handed her one of his cards. "I was hoping to speak with Mr. McInnis, madam."

Her eyes flickered at the card and widened as she recognized his name. The woman ordered a clerk to oversee the shop and beckoned for Daniel to follow her.

"I'm surprised and pleased to see you, my lord. I trust her ladyship is well?"

"I believe so." He hesitated. "Am I speaking with Mrs. McInnis?"

She smiled and gave Daniel a nod. "Aye, your lordship."

The back workshop was busy and full of noise. He looked around at the areas of the print shop and the tasks being performed. He never thought about what went into making the prints. Clearly it was not as simple as he imagined.

Mrs. McInnis knocked on the door of an office. A red-haired man with an ink-stained apron opened the door, smiling at his wife. His smile faltered as Mrs. McInnis lead Daniel into the office and, instead of leaving as Daniel had assumed she would, she followed him in and closed the door behind her.

"My lord, this is my husband, Mr. McInnis. This is his lordship, the earl of Beechingstoke."

"Ah, what can I do for you, my lord?" Mr. McInnis said uncertainly.

Daniel looked from husband to wife and back before he cleared his throat, his nerves getting to him. "It came to my attention that Lady Beechingstoke was keeping all of this"—he waved his hand—"from me."

Mrs. McInnis scoffed. "Of course she did. You're

Lord Beechingstoke. The whole ton is well aware of your views on caricatures."

"Mrs. McInnis, leave the lad alone," Mr. McInnis chided. He turned to Daniel. "Please sit, my lord, and tell us why you've come."

"I'm here to right a wrong." He set Stella's portfolio on Mr. McInnis's table. Taking a breath, Daniel confided in the McInnises about Lady Sinclair's revelation and how he had banished Stella from their London townhome. With every word, he knew the McInnises could use anything he said in a caricature to mock him and Stella, but he suspected they would not.

They sat silent through his story. As he finished, Daniel tapped on the portfolio. "There are caricatures of me in here that her ladyship did not publish. I want you to print them."

The McInnises looked at one another and seemed to have a silent conversation in that way that only couples who knew each another well could do. His heart ached for Stella, and he wondered if they would ever reach that point in their relationship.

Mrs. McInnis pulled the papers out of the portfolio, regarding them before passing them to her husband. He leaned forward and whispered something into her ear that Daniel couldn't quite catch.

With her nod, Mr. McInnis set the pile down and tapped it with his finger. "Are you certain you want these published?"

Daniel nodded without hesitation.

"And I know she supports the Willows with her

proceeds from the caricatures, so please have any funds sent to them."

Mr. McInnis's lips twitched, and he held out his hand. "We can make that happen."

"When will the caricatures be printed?" Daniel asked, eager to be out of the print shop.

"Two days," Mrs. McInnis said.

The men turned to her. Mr. McInnis cocked a brow. "I thought I was in charge of the print schedule."

Mrs. McInnis shrugged. "I'm overruling it. Everyone is wondering about the Beechingstoke marriage. It's the perfect time to display the prints for the best profit."

Daniel's jaw tightened, but he refrained from speaking. While he did not want his marriage as a source for gossip, let alone for profit, he knew that this was the only way to get Stella back. At least he hoped it would work.

CHAPTER TWENTY-ONE

S tella sat on the window seat overlooking the garden at the Redwicks' house and sighed. A sketchbook lay beside her, open to an empty page begging for an idea.

Ideas that would not come.

It had been four long days since she'd last seen Daniel. Her anger had mellowed, and she was overwhelmed with longing. Longing for his smiles, their conversations and to be in his arms again.

She closed her eyes, knowing that she needed to do something, anything, even if it was picking up the pieces of her heart and going to Beechingstoke Manor to begin anew. Without him.

The rustling of skirts at the door had Stella turn as Iris rushed in.

"What in heaven's name are you doing here?" Iris crossed the room and grasped Stella's hand.

Stella's brows furrowed in puzzlement. It wasn't

Iris's at home day, when guests visit. "Did I forget plans?" Iris ignored the question and pulled Stella out of the room, calling for someone to fetch their hats and gloves.

"We're going out on calls?" Stella looked at her gown. It was comfortable, but rather dowdy for morning calls. "I'll just go change."

"There's no time!" Iris said as she led Stella to the door. "We must hurry, before they're all gone."

"What are you talking about?" Stella asked. Cassandra stood in the front entry, bouncing on her heels in excitement. "Cassandra, what are you doing here? What's going on?"

Iris pulled on her gloves and smiled. "Wait and see."

Stella scarcely had time to pull on her gloves before they ushered her into the Redwicks' waiting landau. The top was down so they could enjoy the gorgeous, sunny day. Stella paused. "It seems a bit early to be promenading at the park. Do we need parasols?"

"No!" cried Cassandra.

Iris stepped into the carriage. "Get in."

They took off at a brisk pace. Stella closed her eyes and lifted her face to the sun. It was a lovely, warm day, and she was thrilled to be outdoors. Perhaps Daniel would visit her today.

Stella squashed that thought the moment it formed. Much to her disappointment, Daniel had neither called nor written to her at the Redwicks' house. He knew she was there—Lord Redwick had told her he'd informed Daniel—but he continued to avoid her.

It stung, him not wanting her. So she threw herself into creating silly drawings for the Redwick children and trying not to cry as she witnessed the closeness between their parents.

"Look at this crowd!" Cassandra exclaimed.

Stella opened her eyes, aware that the carriage slowed. She looked around in confusion, her eyes adjusting to the bright light. They were near McInnis's Print Shop, in the opposite direction of the park.

"Why aren't we at the park?" Stella asked, as Iris ordered the horses to be stopped at the same time.

"It'll be easier to walk," Iris reasoned.

"To the park from here? Are you mad?" asked Stella. Perhaps this was an elaborate scheme to force her out of the Redwicks' home—lose her in a crowd and leave her to her own devices.

Stella exited the carriage behind Cassandra. She heard Iris order her driver to move further up the road, before they made their way down the street.

The street was crowded, more crowded than Stella had seen it before. All sorts of people were gathered around the windows of McInnis's Print Shop.

Stella's breath caught in her throat. She wondered if one of her caricatures was the reason for the commotion. What a coup that would be!

"Oh, these are wonderful," one woman laughed.

"It's a shame most men are like that," another grumbled.

Stella moved closer and froze. Several of her caricatures of Daniel, the ones she'd never published, stood proudly in the window display.

"I like that one!" Cassandra pointed at a caricature.

"How did they get these?" Stella asked in horror. Daniel would be mortified.

"I gave them to McInnis." A low voice, so achingly familiar, spoke from behind Stella, and she turned.

He stood behind her, looking so handsome and apprehensive as he shifted from foot to foot in the crowd.

"Daniel," she whispered. Caricatures forgotten, she took a step towards him. She took his outstretched hand and allowed him to lead her away from the crowd.

He dropped her hand and scratched the back of his neck. "Stella, I owe you an apology. I was an ass, and there was no excuse for my behaviour—"

"You banished me." She crossed her arms in a protective gesture. "Do you have any idea how that feels? To be forced away from you and our new life?"

"Perhaps as much as you keeping such a large secret from me," Daniel replied, hurt in his voice. "When were you going to tell me? Why did I have to hear it from someone else?"

Stella opened her mouth in anger and forced it closed. She took a breath, knowing that they needed to have this conversation now. "I could see how hurt you'd been when you spoke of the other caricatures. I was scared... I thought you would push me away if I told you. Lady Sinclair told me she'd give me a week to tell you. Instead, she told you early. I was going to tell you that night, but then you..." She lifted and dropped her hand, not wanting to relive the memory of their argument.

He took her hands in his. "I'm sorry. I said horrible things that night that I regret. After our fight, I went up to your studio. I saw your work, Stella. I really saw it."

He closed his eyes. When he opened them, they were full of tears. "I was wrong. I had no right to banish or threaten you the way I did. Your work is as much a part of you as... as your hands." Daniel brought her hands up to his lips and kissed them. "Forbidding you from drawing would be like breaking off your hands. I know that now. I will never ask you to make such a sacrifice again."

Tears welled in Stella's eyes. She swallowed the lump in her throat.

She felt him kiss her wet cheek and whisper her name before enfolding her into his arms.

Stella burrowed in close, savouring the feel and scent of this man, her husband.

The sound of clapping startled Stella. She pulled her head from Daniel's chest and turned to see Cassandra with her hands clasped together, a wide grin on her face and Iris clapping.

"Does this mean you're leaving us?" Iris asked. She stuck out her lower lip in a pout. "The children will be devastated."

Stella's laugh was watery. "It's not like I'll be far."

"Cassandra!" Everyone winced as the shrill tones sounded above the crowd. Stella stiffened as she watched Lady Sinclair make her way towards them. Her ladyship narrowed her eyes as she took in the scene in front of her. "What are you doing out here in the street?"

"Hello, Mother!" Cassandra greeted with a forced cheer. "How did you know where to find me?"

"Your mother has some one following you." Everyone turned to Stella.

Cassandra gasped and whirled on her mother. "How dare you! I have been properly chaperoned by the lady's maid and footman you insist on sending with me. To have more people following me? What are you afraid of?"

Lady Sinclair pointed at Stella and hissed. "That woman is corrupting you. If you had any sense, you would have listened to me and been a dutiful daughter. You could have been the one compromised in the library at Lady Harrington's, not her."

Silence fell around them. Stella looked from mother to daughter before she stepped forward and clasped Cassandra's hand in hers.

"Good day, my lady." Stella nodded towards the print shop, ignoring Lady Sinclair's previous statement. "Have you seen the latest prints?"

Daniel laughed. "They're some of my favourites. My wife is rather talented, is she not, my lady? And we've decided to keep her identity a secret."

"It will be a secret, my lord." Cassandra promised.

"If word gets out from my mother, then I will create such a scandal that she'll never be able to show her face in polite society again."

Lady Sinclair's jaw dropped. Something passed between mother and daughter. Her shoulders slumped. "Well. I suppose it's for the best."

Cassandra stepped towards her mother, sliding her arm around her. "Come mother, you appear fatigued. It's time we go home."

Without another word, she and her mother disappeared into the crowd.

Daniel cleared his throat and picked up Stella's hand. "I find caricatures have grown on me. Particularly Mr. Starr's. I look forward to seeing more of them."

Stella's heart skipped. His eyes met hers, and she could see how serious he was. His support was everything she had ever wished for. She knew in that moment exactly what she needed to do.

"I love you, Daniel," she whispered as she kissed his cheek.

He pulled her in close again and murmured those same three words before covering her mouth with his.

"This is better than a play!" Iris sighed, dabbing the tears from her eyes.

Stella buried her face in his chest in embarrassment.

"Come," she heard him whisper, "let's go home."

S tella curled her arms around the box and clutched it like one would hold a child. It contained one of the greatest treasures Stella had to offer: her new book.

She hurried to Daniel's study and knocked on the door, shifting her weight from one foot to the other as she waited for him to answer. Stella was excited and anxious to show off the book.

Daniel sat at his desk, a neat stack of correspondence piled in front of him. He gave Stella a smile as he stood to greet her.

"It's done!" Stella exclaimed as she crossed the room. She set the box onto Daniel's desk with a flourish. "Will you open it?"

He set aside his correspondence and pulled the box towards him. One eyebrow arched at Stella as she squeezed her hands together in anticipation.

"Are you sure you want me to open it?" Daniel asked.

Stella nodded, too eager and impatient to do it herself.

Daniel pinched a string of the bow and pulled. The bow uncurled and fell off the package. He set aside the string and pulled off the box lid. Tissue paper lay below. Daniel scooped it up, crumpled it into a ball, and tossed it at Stella with a grin.

"Enough! Just get to the book, Daniel!" Stella begged.

"Patience, love." Daniel chuckled, clearly enjoying Stella's anxiety.

He pulled out the book. It was bound in dark blue leather and embossed in gold lettering:

Caricatures of a Countess—A year in the life of Lady D, by Mr. E. Starr

Daniel frowned as Stella reached over to reverently trace the letters with her fingertips. "Who the devil is Lady D?"

"I couldn't exactly use my name, Daniel!" Stella protested. "Besides, we've only been wed for a few months, not a year."

Daniel fumbled around his desk before grabbing a penknife and the book. He stood and walked out of the room. Stunned, it took Stella a moment to follow Daniel down the hall and into the library.

He sat on the settee, patting the space beside him,

"May as well be comfortable as I inspect how the ton will view our marriage."

Stella tried hard not to roll her eyes. The caricatures were nothing like their marriage—well, not really. There might be some similarities, but nothing that most of the ton could identify them by. Or at least that's what Stella hoped.

Daniel opened his penknife to cut open the first page. He continued in this manner, slicing where the pages met, opening to the drawings, and examining each and every one.

Stella peered over his shoulder, silent but not still. It was amazing, she thought, that he could concentrate with her practically bouncing on the settee.

He read through the entire volume without saying a word. When he finished, he gently set the book on to the table in front of them and turned to Stella.

She held her breath, awaiting his verdict. Everyone else in the world could hate the book. The only opinion she cared for was his.

"You're very talented, Mr. Starr."

Stella broke out into a blinding grin. "Do you really think so?"

Daniel cocked a brow. "It's brilliant, Stella. It was funny and clever. I particularly liked the drawing of the couple in the library. It was... familiar."

"I'm glad you enjoyed it," Stella replied primly.

"I was wrong to believe that your work was harmful. It's not. You bring laughter to an uncertain world." Daniel's smile faded as he grasped her hand. In a more serious tone he asked, "I'm sorry I let your caricatures come between us. Do you forgive me?"

Stella closed her eyes and inhaled deeply. His acceptance meant more to her than she thought it would. Memories of their courtship and the early days of their marriage flashed in her mind. There were so many misunderstandings and troubles, it was amazing that they made it this far, together.

She opened her eyes. The love of her life filled her vision. "I forgive you, Daniel. I forgave you long ago."

He grinned and gave her a quick kiss. "That's my countess. So, what is your next project?"

Stella's grin returned. "Another book about Lady D. This time I was thinking Lady D travels to Brighton or the Lake District? I'll need someone to take me there for research. Do you know anyone?" She batted her lashes flirtatiously at him.

Daniel wrapped his arms around Stella and pulled her in close. Her eyes closed as he nuzzled her neck. It was wonderful to be in his arms.

"How about Lady B goes upstairs with her husband?"

Stella laughed and pulled back to look Daniel in the eyes. "Who says we need to go upstairs when we can have our next adventure right here?"

"Clever countess of mine," Daniel murmured as he leaned into Stella and deepened their kiss.

The End

WANT TO READ A DELETED SCENE FROM CARICATURE OF A COUNTESS?

Thank you for reading Caricature of a Countess! I hope you loved reading Daniel and Stella's story as much as I loved writing it.

Please feel free to leave a review wherever you purchased this book from. Reviews help other readers discover books.

Want to read a deleted scene from Caricature of a Countess?
Go to https://authormelissasawyer.com/coc-deleted-scene
to sign up for my newsletter and receive a copy of a deleted scene from Caricature of a Countess.

ACKNOWLEDGMENTS

My critique partners and those offering me feedback - Leanna, Patricia, Randi, Celeste, Caralyn, Molly, Abigail, Sarah, Laura, Christie and Vanessa. Your suggestions have been so valuable for this book.

My editor, Sarah, thank you for your insights, patience and making me laugh with your comments. You've helped me so much during this new experience.

Holly, for my gorgeous cover.

The Toronto Romance Writers Sunday morning write-in group - Blake, Laura, Julie, Jessica, and everyone else who joined in. Thank you for being there to motivate me.

The Toronto Romance Writers and the Regency Fiction Writers groups – thank you for being a place for me to learn and grow the past few years.

My mother, Donna, for being my alpha reader and biggest cheerleader.

My kids, even though you still have several years before you can read this book. Thank you for telling your friends that your mom wrote a book that is inappropriate to talk about at the dinner table, and for always asking me when the book would be finished.

RESOURCES

The following are some of the many resources have inspired this book:

The Tour of Doctor Syntax by William Combe

Information about Mrs Charlotte Turner Smith, her Poem # 70, and more about her work
>   https://doi.org/10.1093/ref:odnb/25790
>   Poem LXX (70)
>   https://quod.lib.umich.edu/b/bwrp/SmitCElegi/1:11.78?rgn=div2;view=fulltext

James Gillray, caricature artist and information about print sellers
>   https://james-gillray.org/printsellers.html

ABOUT THE AUTHOR

Melissa Sawyer lives in Toronto, Canada with her husband and three children. When she is not writing you can find her reading, cross stitching, listening to music or gardening on her balcony.

Caricature of a Countess is her first book.